The Book

Adam, grew up without any worries or cares, didn't take life too seriously. Up till now that is, now he has to face up to responsibility. That he's in a position now to use magic makes him insecure.
But with Emiliana as his guardian at his side, he's ready to start his journey of great adventure full of resentment, war and sorrow, but also true love.

The Author
Born in 1969 in Schwerin, The father of 3 children, Uwe Balzeriet lives a small town called Güstrow in Mecklenburg Vorpommern. Inspired by his own campfire stories over the holidays and at junior film camps. He has now put those magical stories down on paper and they are called (tbd)

Aridas World

Part 1

Ellion
Uwe Balzereit
2017

Binding and mapping : www.gregor-reisch.de
Picture Art : Sabrina Pahlke
Copy-editing : www.mandy-kommoss.de
Translated by Marie O´Donnell

Bibliographic Information from the German National
Library.
The German National Library listed this Publication in
the German National Bibliography, detailed
Bibliographic data are available online at dnb.dnb.de

TWENTYSIX- Der Self Publishing - Verlag
Eine Kooperation zwischen der Verlagsgruppe Random
House und

BoD-Books on Demand
© 2017 Uwe Balzereit

Herstellung und Verlag BoD - Book on Demand,
Norderstedt

ISBN 9783740764654

For Josephine

Prologue

It was loud in the Great Hall. The person standing at the speakers desk tried in vain to let herself be heard, over the drone of voices. With the help of magic she watched the commotion before her, and proceeded in an inhuman loud voice: >> Quuuiet! Now listen!<< Suddenly the Counsel went silent. All eyes were on Olidir, the Counsel Elder. >>Now listen to me! The prophecy tells us exactly what is to be done. Progress and Development in this form must not happen! We cannot allow another Wizard to ever get this powerful again. Towns folk were destroyed, as we allowed one of our own to call upon powers, that were out of their control.

We allowed our collective knowledge to be abused. It has been foretold, that another such wizard will rise. Therefore we will intervene this time and keep a watchful eye on his development and on those who are associated with him.

 Olidir looked around him. Nearly all the seats in the Great Hall were occupied. Wizards from all worlds where gathered here.

The High Counsel called them here upon hearing of a War of the Deamons, in which millions would fall. Only through level-headedness and working together, did they manage to win over the bad and cleanse all the portals. Portals that creatures darker than night broke through. That brought nothing but destruction and death.

Olidir arose to speak again>> I put forth that the Book of Elements be split in two. The ballot will determine who will guard them. I recommend also that the Pixie Staff be brought back under the protection of the Pixies, and The Sword of Trunan should also be returned to its place of origin Black Rock. Henceforth the Fortress of curses will now be the stronghold for that person who seeks only to use magic to do good. Here we will learn to direct and improve magic for the greater good of all worlds.<<

Whispers made their way through the rows. Most nodded in silent approval.

The Counsel of Elders arose and so it was set. From now on ARIDA would be completely cut off from the rest. ARIDA would be observed and directed by all the Wizards here in the Fortress of the Curses.

Here begins the story of boy not yet a man, in a world, in which time brought forth strange things. In a world full of Magic and peril, that would change the life of anyone.

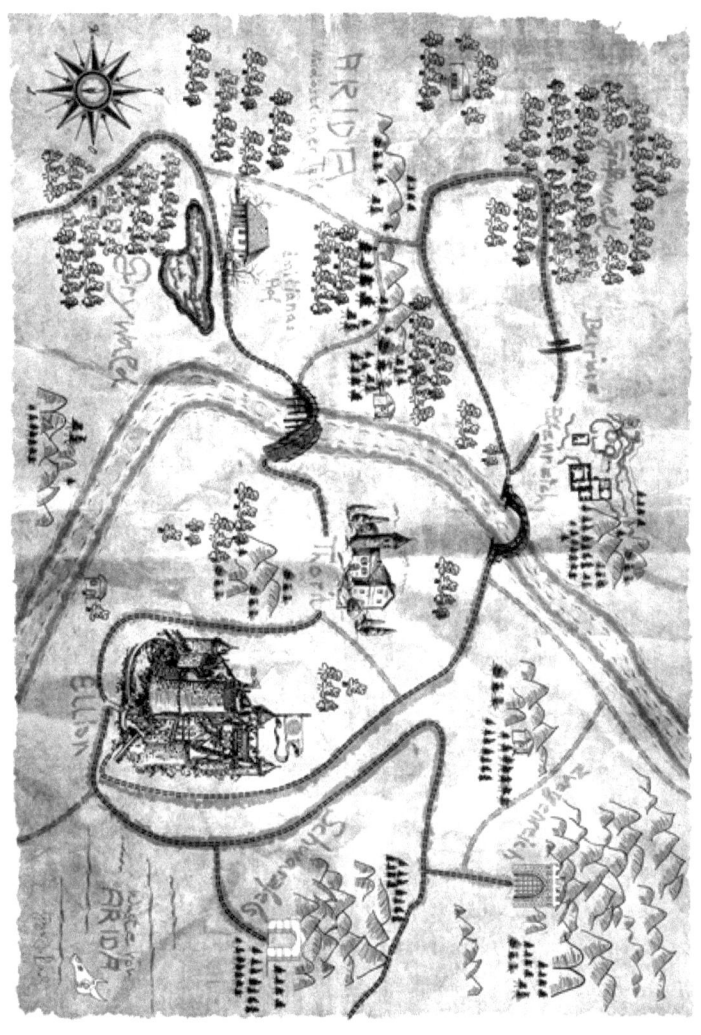

Farions Story

The night was young. Yet it was time to put down the work and rest up for the next day. The fading sun was still visible on the horizon. The sky was coloured gold yellow to deep red. Even the wind had died down and the Swallows were gliding through the air over the calm lake, to catch some insects, which were now swarming in abundance. The Village was too small and cut off, so that no-one would ever find themselves lost here. Even the traders only came here once a year. Cut off from all the progressions that the world has experienced, it seemed as though time stood still in this village.

The villagers had seemed forgotten and that over several generations.

As a white speck on the map of the Realm they were left to fend for themselves, and spent their lives with their own community. Not every village had a teller that travelled far and wide and could pass on hid stories of adventure, but Henry, one of the Elders was known for his stories, that he always told as though they had happened to him.

The others made themselves comfortable, and stretched out their tired legs. The lingering warmth from the sun could still be felt, yet

there was already a mighty fire burning. The wood was crackling and spitting out little worms of glowing ember into the air. A Lyra was quietly playing music, as the kettle hanging over the flames gave off delicious scents of its own. Pitchers of wine and other sweet smelling drinks made their rounds. Here in the village everyone had to pull together to make it through the harsh winter. The crop stock was not looking good after the last two harvests did not go so well. That was not allowed to happen again. So the remaining growing crops of grain and vegetables were well tended to.
So tonight the villagers where enjoying a night of rest bite by the fire after a long day of hard work. The time had come for Henry to tell his tale.

You wouldn't believe it. A long time ago an event took place in this village that only the elders will remember. There once lived a young lad here in our village, by the name of Adam. Adam was about 20 years young, and was quite the attraction to the ladies here. With his brown hair and green eyes they saw something special in him. Instead of going to work he spent his days pursuing the ladies and showering them with profound language. It didn't take long for him to get a bad reputation. One night in the Tavern one of the villagers found out that Adam was pursuing his daughter, and not with honourable intentions, but with a promise of "adventure" as he liked to put it. The father stumbled out of the tavern in a drunken rage, thanks to a generous amount of beer, with the intention of having words with Adam, after all enough was enough !!! His daughter was promised to someone else, the wedding already registered and displayed at the Town Hall.

There! Adam was walking across the town square, smarty dressed with a neat hair cut, as he was known.

The old man yelled >> Hey you! ADAM!<< Adam spun round at the sound of the voice that was calling out to him. >> Oh no! Undines Father!<< Adam could already tell by the look on his face that his mood was not to be messed with. He picked up his steps, as he was not strong enough to deal with a man in that kind of state, he knew better and wanted to get out of his way. Undines father was seething with rage >>You boy, will not get away from me! Today is the day you pay!<< Adam was shocked at how quickly the old man caught up to him, and at that moment had already gotten a hold of him and threw him to the ground. Laboured he pulled himself up, Adam was fear stricken.

The old man shouted >> God help you, if I ever see you near my daughter ever again!<<

Adam replied >>But I love your daughter!<<
His voice was scratchy like that of a little boy.
>>You think you love her?<< asked the father.
>> You just want to have your fun and then be gone. That stops now!
 You will not further put a stain on this family!<<
Meanwhile the other villagers had noticed to commotion. Candles were lit and shop shutters opened to see what was going on. Undines mother came rushing and started pulling at her husband. >> Come home! Yet again you have drank too much!<< she said resentfully.

Undines father was beside himself >>I need to sort this out! Undine is promised to someone else and this good for nothing boy needs to keep away!<<
Adam brushed off his clothes and smoothed them down, looking around at the people that had gathered around them. >> Oh man<<, he thought to himself, >> How am I going to get myself out of this mess?<<, just as Undine was walking straight towards him.
 Just as she stood before him, her hand already flying through the air open fisted, connecting right in the middle of his face.
>>You deserved that!<<, she yelled as her voice boomed. "Making pretty eyes at me, whilst you've got a thing with Emiliana on the side!?"

Adams face reddened, the only area of pure white where Undines hand had connected with his face.

As this pure white was turning to a deep red, Adam was realising his way out of this. Adam turned to Undines parents, who had watched the scene unfold in amazement. >>I promise to stay away from your daughter!<< And Undine, he turned to face her. >>It would never have worked between us, your parents would never have given us their blessing. Please forgive me!<< He turned on his heel and disappeared into the darkness.

Undine broke into tears.

She really did love   Adam, and now to be embarrassed in front of all these villagers.

Undines mother was dumb struck put came out of it to take her daughter in her arms and lead her home while trying to comfort her.

Undines father followed them home with a light stagger.

With this the town square began to empty, and the peace returned.

Shop shutters were closed with a squeak and the lights extinguished.

Silence fell over the village as night began to set in.

The Promise

Emiliana please just believe me ! Its not what
you think ! I love you and want to marry you !
Please understand ! I know you cant trust me
after what happened last night, but please try
and believe me, I love you and only you !
Please Emiliana, please !
He lay at Emilianas feet, tears streaming down
his face. Emiliana gently pushed him from her.
>> I think it would be better, if we didn't see
each other any more .<<
Desperate now Adam takes her hand and
looks her deep in the eyes. Begging now >>
Please believe me!<<
>>Why is he doing this to me?<< She thought
desperately trying to understand.
Of course she liked Adam, yet there was
barely a single woman in the village who
hadn't heard the same promises from him.
How was she going to find out that he meant
it with her ? She opened his hand, removed
her own hand and spoke: >> Adam try and
better yourself and show me that you can stay
loyal to me. For this I give you 3 months, and
will wait for you. Should nothing change by
then, however, I will be finished with you. I
would even set the village Mayor on you ! So
think about who and what is important to

you.<< With these words she straightened her skirt and went home, leaving Adam standing there puzzled.

>>Oh, what am I going to do?<< Adam thought to himself. He liked her green eyes , those eyes that enthralled him right from the start, her soft black curls and her slim form. But to give up his life for that ? To change everything and grow up, for that ?

Arriving home he was confused. Everywhere stood boxes, bags and big suitcases.

>>What's all this?<< He shouted >> What is going on here?<<

His father came out of the kitchen. >> My Boy we are going to move to town, as I have accepted a position at the University as a lecturer, and am allowed to further my own knowledge of the sciences. Your mother is already there to get things set up for us. You will enrol with me and make something of it. Far too long have I stood by and watched as you throw your life away!<<

Is Adam dreaming? Was everything going under ? What was actually going on ? Confused he looked around. No it wasn't a dream. His live was actually changing.

>>EMILIANA<<, he thought suddenly. >> Father! NO! Please, you cant do this to me!<< He shouted full of despair.

Adams father looked through his papers with his small glasses. The sun shinning on his ever polished gleaming glasses frame. His face distorted showing everything but joy. Adam understood.

>>Father please, just give me 3 months, then I will gladly go with you and start my studies for sure. I have something very important here that I need to get sorted first.<< He begged.

>>OK, fine.<< He said. >>But I need to start with my experiments and thus we will only see each other at the weekends. In the meantime you can stay in the village. But you will take the last transport, not a day later!<< During dinner Adam tapped his fingers on the table nervously, and pushed the food around with his fork without taking notice.

>>Adam what's wrong? What's on your mind?<< Asked his father. >>Oh nothing, I was just lost in my thoughts.<< He answered. >>I will get this daydreaming of yours out of you as soon as you're in town with me. Now eat. I will be on the road for 7 days and let me tell you the food will certainly not be this good. After you can help load up the rest of the gear! This work isn't going to do itself!<< Adam went out the front reluctantly, where he loaded what seemed like an endless load of boxes and suitcases. The helpers clothes were sticking to them from the sweat from all the hard work, the dust sticking to their skin,

making them look more like chimney sweeps than anything else.

>>What are you staring at?<< Big beads of sweat running down the face of the big man standing before him. >>Don't just stand there and start helping before I make you!<<

Adam double quick, made his way to a big pile of boxes and carried them to the wagon. The big man also made his way back over, grumbling all the while. Adam regretted having put on clean clothes. After a short time he was already full of dust and sweat.

To add insult to injury Adam had ripped his shirt, as one of the big wooden boxes had slipped out of his hand. A hand connected with the back of head with someone shouting: >>You idiot, cant even do that right!<<

After the work was done Adam rushed to his room to take another look around. >>His room<<, he thought. It was as empty as his life. Even the big wooden wardrobe he had already crawled on as a child, with its flowery patterns and fine etchings, in which he used to hide as a child stood behind the chair, that now only holds the few items of clothing he needs for the journey. How was he going to leave all this behind in just 3 months time ? He would miss all those many years he had spent here. Adam hadn't noticed yet, that first step to adulthood had been made.

The weeks went by. Working day in and day out made the time fly. >> 10 Days is all that is left, then the 3 months are up<< Thought Adam. >>But how am I supposed to explain to Emiliana that I must leave? How can I convince her to come with me? Will she even believe me? And what would father say?<< All these questions constantly on his mind.
Sure Father Malkier had his place at the University. Even during the weekends they had spent together, his father spent leaning over papers and mumbled things like >> My creations they will be... Tools of power they will be... All will kneel before me...!<<
Adam started to doubt his fathers sanity, as well as his mother who was also worried. Malkier had a bad reputation at the University, he was too strict with his students, worked mainly on his experiments and didn't stick to the course plans. >>What could it be, that has changed him so much? If only we had stayed in the village my darling son.<< she had once said to Adam. Though he did get lots of tasks from his father, they had nothing to do with his studies, with his own major. His training had more to do with being his father errand boy than an actual qualification of any sort. Adam was never allowed to be there for any of the research, he was always made to leave the laboratory before any of it began. >>Father, why don't you let me

contribute?<< He asked one day. >>How am I supposed to learn your research if I am never allowed to watch?<< Adams father turned to face him, his face one of pure angry annoyance. Adam knew this meant nothing good. >>If I tell you to go, then you go!<< he shouted. His ever pristine hair fell over his face, giving him the look of a crazy man. Adam was shocked. Never has he seen his father like this. >>Then do your things on your own from now own!<< Adam shouted back. >>You only live for your research. We, mother and me and everyone else, just don't matter to you any more. I´m leaving father!<< Malkier shook with anger. Mad he swept everything off his desk with one arm. Equipment fell to the floor with a bang and glass flew through the air. Assorted chemicals made their way over the floor with the steam rising along the way. >> Get out of my sight you good for nothing. You show me no respect and doubt my abilities? OUT! I dont ever want to see you here again!<< Throwing his arms about as he shouted at Adam and even threw his pen after him, leaving a blot of ink on the wall where it hit. Adam slammed the door behind him and thought: What on earth was that ? That was not his father. What ever has happened to him? Even though he was always strict, he always had time for his family . How could he have changed this much in 3 months? Now he understood why he heard his mother crying silently on many a night. Without even realising he had arrived at home. His mother opened the door to him, holding a piece of paper in her hands and tears in her eyes. >>Mother what's wrong? What's happened? Why are you crying?<< >>Oh Adam<<, Sobbing she embraced Adam tight. >>What have you got there?<< Silently she handed Adam the letter. It had the university logo on it.

Honourable Professor

Again we must ask you to leave and clear the laboratory. You have not been granted permission to further use the equipment you have, yet you continue to use these after you have been made to resign 4 weeks ago now. The open sum of 13,000 crowns are to be payed in full. Should you not comply, we will be forced to repossess your belongings to that amount.

Sincerely
Privy Counsellor Märtens
University Doctor
Adam was speechless. What had his father done? He looked to his mother, who was slumped in her chair, hands in her lap nestling her tear soaked tissue. >> My son I do not know. Your father has used up all our

savings on his experiments. We are nearly broke.<< Again she began to sob. >>Mother we are going home. Come on, pack your most important things!<< Adams mother looked up. >>What do you mean, home? This is our home now.<< Adam turned to face his mother, and knelt before her, so he could look into her eyes. He took her face in his hands and said earnestly >> Mother this was never our home. Father wanted it like this, but we never belonged here.<< She handed Adam a Glace leather purse, it was very elegant and had a Golden clasp. >>My boy, take this and go.<< Adam opened the purse. She jumped up with a crack. She was laden with papers, title deeds to a piece of land in the woods with buildings close to the lake, and also a whole lot of crowns. Adam jumped in shock. >>Mother what is the meaning of this? Where did this come from and why are you giving it to me?<< She looked at him sad. >> I cannot leave here son. I have too mind your father. You are old enough. Now take your things and leave! You will find a map that will show you the way. We will see each other again. I love you.<< Tears streamed down her face and Adam tried to disguise his sadness. So much can change in such a short time, he lost his house, his father and now too his mother. He was to go on, alone. >>No!<< He thought. >>I will take Emiliana with me. I need to go to her. I cannot loose her too!<< Even though he was in turmoil, such where his thoughts. He must return to the village and return to the calm, because here in town everything was different. The many people, all those lights in the night, the strange machines, that moved as though through magic through the streets to transport the people. He had never got to notice that time in his village had stood still for near 2 hundred years. Those people in town gave him strange glances because of his clothing, that didn't match their new trends. His vocabulary and way of speaking sounded as though from a different time and as such he was laughed at often because of it. It didn't bother Adam too much, although sometimes it did hurt. Town confused him and he was happy to be leaving all that behind him. "Let them progress as they will." He thought. "I'm going home! I´m going to Emiliana!"

That was his motivation. Tomorrow he would buy himself a car and drive home. The people of the village will be amazed, that he, a good fr nothing , would return and arrive in a car of all things. The journey took 7 days. It was a hard and tiring journey, though Adam didn't care. He was going to see his Emiliana and that was all that mattered to him.

Demons

Nothing had changed. Everything looked as though he had never left. He took a room at the local Inn. >>Can you even pay for it?<< Asked the Inn keeper. Adam handed him 10 crowns in advance. >>That's enough for 5 days including meals. Upstairs first room to your left.<< Said the host as he disappeared into the kitchen. >>Great welcome!<< Thought Adam. He ordered a bath, then food and then a beer.

Now clean and fed he left the Inn. He wanted to see what had become of the village. >>Oh our Adam has become a Fine Sir<<, Joked the local blacksmith Lorin. >> And so smartly dressed! Which pretty head are you hoping to turn today then?<< He laughed and went back to his work. Others also turned their heads and whispered among themselves, though this didn't bother Adam a bit. Many of his friends weren't there, some had begun their studies and other had gone off travelling. So Adam returned to the Inn. The bar was very popular during this time. Flames dancing in the fire, beside it sat a Bard singing songs of far away lands, with flying machines and so on. At the next table cards were being played but not exactly quietly. Adam sat in the corner, ordered himself a beer and listened to the music. It was very rare to the see a Bard here. Marie served the guests and then made her way over to Adam asking >>Would you perhaps like something to eat Adam?<< She looked at him with such kind eyes as she leaned down to him and said >>I will gladly always be there for you.<<

>>Oh, erm, no no<<, he murmured >>No thanks, I have eaten already, I will take another beer that's it thanks.<< His face now bright red.

>> Now now don't play shy, my dear Adam, your reputation precedes you. I'm sure a bit of fun would do us both good!<< Marie grinned longingly at him. >> I, I'm taken. Just a beer please.>> Marie laughing now, >>The philanderer is taken, how cute!<< Her laugh had turned to grimace, and five minutes later she slammed the beer on his table and left him sitting there. Adam drank his beer. This day had been too much for him. As he was taking his leave to his room more than several pairs of eyes stared after him and not in a good way either.

The next morning he had a note sent to Emiliana. >> My love, please meet me tonight at the lake, right after sundown at our old spot. Love Your Adam.<<

Feeling different than usual Adam felt that today time was standing still. He could think of nothing else other than his meeting with Emiliana. He spent the whole day at the Inn in his room. His bed laden with all the papers his mother had given him. Many of the documents already very old with seal stamps and bands around them. He had even found the map. It showed a building with woods at a lake, maybe 30 days or so away from the village. His mother had never told him of this place. But why? But now was not the time to dwell on these thoughts. He gathered the papers together and hid them in his room. Finally! The evening drew nearer. His excitement kept growing. Many of the villagers bowed their heads and giggled as they say Adam strolling though the village dressed up to the nines. >> I heard he was moving to town to live with his father<<, said one elderly woman. >>Yes there he will have no shortage of love interests. He is a good for nothin and always will be!<< said another. >>But why is he living in the Inn?<< Undines mother asked. >>What he is doing back here?<<

Adam could feel the eyes on him. He tried not to run but his step kept quickening. He just wanted to get to Emiliana, finally a new life with her. He was shaking with excitement, heart beating so fast he was almost sure the others could hear it. Nervous as he was he almost ran the last few steps to the rendezvous point.

Just a little further, past the three giant trees, that had been there forever, even as he had started to learn to walk, and had even then seemed so tall and eerie as soon as the sun had went down.

The grass already wet, his shoes glistening with the little water drops and the cold already creeping though the material. But all this didn't interest him in the slightest. Adam only had one goal: Emiliana!

Then there she was! His heart skipped a beat from all the excitement and all he had in him was joy. Fear was also amongst the joy, fear that she could show him the cold shoulder again, and remain stubborn.

She raised a hand and waved him over. A few steps was all it took for Adam to be beside her. Yet he struggled to get the words out though all the restlessness, all he had managed to mumble was >>Hello. Hey you er em nice to see you again...<< Emiliana looked at him anew and asked >>Is that all you've got to say? What's wrong? You're acting as if I am a ghost.<< It took all Adam had to say. >> Apologies, you're right. Please listen to me. I have done everything you asked of me, everything!<< Emiliana raised an eyebrow but continued to listen. Now he was telling her everything that had happened and ended with the words >>The only thing that matters to me, is you...<<

A smile spread across her face. >>Adam Malkier. You have wised up. What an achievement!<< Adam wasn't quite sure what to make of her words, but Emiliana was already on her way over to him, giving him a lasting and longing kiss. He never wanted to let her go ever again.

>> So does that mean, I mean, that you have decided ? That we...<< Adam didn't know what he wanted to say any more.

>>Yes, you dummy! Yeess!<< she said once more with emphasis on the yes. >> But should you even so much as look at another woman, it will not end well for you!<< She threatened earnestly. Adam was relieved. Now he had won her over all for himself, finally!

But now he had to go after his inheritance. He had after all promised his mother he would. Emiliana saw something was bothering him. >> What's wrong Adam? What's on your mind? Don't tell me you're getting cold feet after all?<<

>>No no, of course not, its just I ´need to return to my mother yard soon and that means I must leave you again, which I of course do not want to do.<< Saddened he bowed his head.

>> That sounds like an adventure. You don't want to do all that without me do you?<< She asked him with a dirty grin on her face. Adam perked up instantly. >>You would really come with me ? But it is so far away, the map said something about 30 days if I even read it right!<<

>>Ah what's 30 days?<< she asked and let him melt from her smile. >> When are we leaving?<< She shouted. >>Tomorrow morning.<< He answered swiftly. Emilianas eyes widened. >> Even though you didn't what would become of us?>> She asked with scepticism in her voice. >> I had to play the hand I was dealt, what else could I do?<< He looked at her apologetic. >> Ok, the come and pick me up tomorrow morning!<< she said walking towards the shore of the lake. She jumped off the dock and into a boat that had been tied up there. The boat had been there for as long she could remember. It belonged to the local fisherman named Roman and was locked up. Although everyone knew where the key was hidden.

As such many people used the boat for many an adventure, but always returned it in one piece and locked it up proper again.

Roman knew his boat was being used as a love nest but this didn't bother him. He liked the young folk. Adam climbed to her in the boat and she paddled a bit away from the shore. It

was a quiet night. There was no wind and no sounds to be heard. So quiet it was eerie. Adam lay the oar to the side, Emiliana rested her head on his shoulder. She was shacking and he could feel that she had cramped up.
>>What's wrong? Are you cold?<<
Her hand squeezed his so hard, that even in the dark her white knuckles could be seen. >> Emiliana! What is it?>> He cried out, as to him it seemed she couldn't hear him.
Suddenly she jumped up a cried out, her eyes widening in terror. Then he strength gave out and she crumbled.
Adam looked out on the water, just a black creature emerged from it. In the dark it was hard to recognise anything, yet Adam knew it had to be big as it was standing in the deep water near to him.
He ducked in the last second as he saw a flash of something. He could hear the hiss of a sword, which flew over his head with unimaginable speed. Then the boat began to teeter as a second creature emerged and tried to grab for Emiliana at the stern of the boat. Instinct kicked in and Adam reached for the oar which he used to swing at the black creature until it let go grumbling all the while. Then it hit him like lightening. The burning pain searing through his leg, as he started to feel the warm blood trickling down his leg. Shook up he looked around. Emiliana still out

cold. As the blade emerged once more and threatened to decapitate him, did Adam reach for the oar and swung with all his might. The sheer force knocking him off his feet.

And again the blade connected with the boat sending wood pieces flying everywhere. >>So this is how it ends?<< Adam rolled over on his other side in despair, punching the side of the boat, just a large bat struck the boat shattering it with a loud crash. Water forced its way in and it began to sink. As the cold and wet started surrounding him he heard a low buzzing that quickly got louder,and with a dull thud drove an arrow into the creature. The creature was thrown back and fell lifeless back into the water. At that same moment the second creature was struck and was now sinking with the remains of the boat. Adam followed the events as if in a trance. He turned Emiliana over and pulled her in the water. The boat now completely gone. He swam with her toward the shore. His leg was bleeding profusely, but the unbearable pain and his worry for Emiliana were the only thing keeping him from passing out. Near the shore now he felt helping hands pulling them both ashore. Then everything around him went black.

Help in the Night

He´s going to die. Just look at him. The wound is as black as night and is infected.<< Said Tinus, a man with a cross as wide as a trunk. He was about 30 years young, a wore a black bear like the northern men.

>>No<<, replied Sven, >> I say we go and get the Healer. She will be able t help him. You know there two are important!<<

>>He´s not going to make it! What about the girl? Is she injured?<<

Sven with his small slightly bent legs went over to Emiliana and leant over her. >>She´s breathing and I don´t see any injuries! Hm she´s a good looking one! Pretty...<<.

>>Sven you´re supposed to be checking her and not undressing her!<< Sven took his hands off the woman. >> Pah, its all for the good of the anatomy!<< Tinus laughed loudly. >> Yeh yeh, but you don´t even know what that means! Now help them and make some Tee!<< Sven turned grimacing to face him. >>What am I your servant? Always on the little one...<< The rest of that sentence was murmured quietly to himself, as he started to set about getting a fire started.

Adam ripped his eyes open. Everything within him felt like it was burning, he only managed

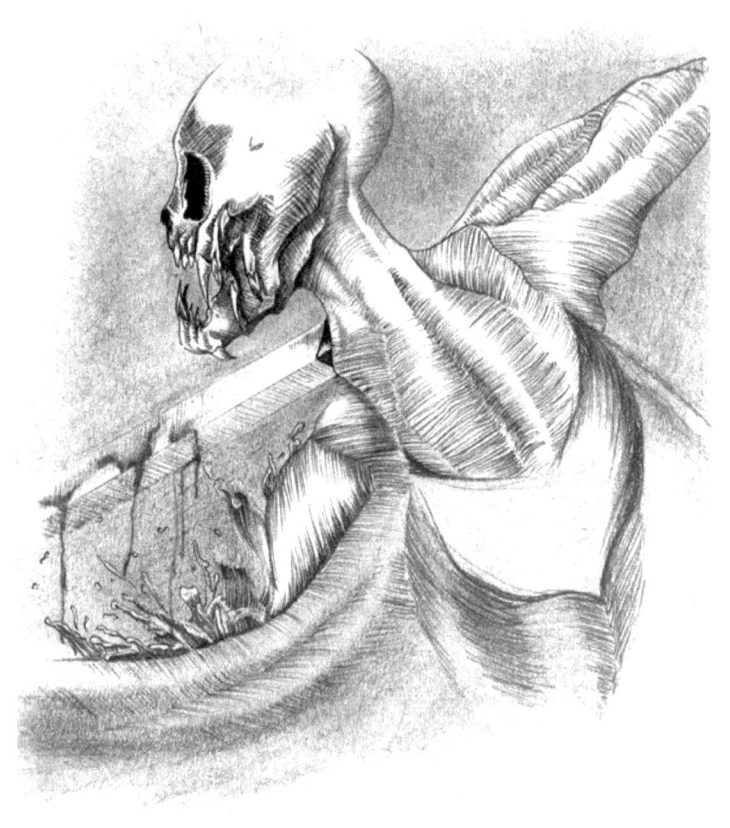

to utter a small whimper. Sweat dripping into his eyes distorting his vision further.

>>Please help, just help me...<< His eyes searching for Emiliana, but she was nowhere to be seen.

Tinus came towards him. >>You were lucky, even though it wasnt very much. You were hurt by a Dangan, their venom will bring you death. Make your piece with the world.<<

>>Go and get the Healer, she can help him, I just know it!<< Shouted Sven across to them, as he was dunking the herbs in the pot of boiling water.

The nice smells filling the air.

Tinus gave in and left, taking long strides along the way into the darkness. >>Ok, i´ll go if it´ll make you happy. Your bad mood is starting to get on my nerves Sven!<<

Only several moments he returned to the fire with a woman, wearing nothing but a black robe and a big ring in the form of a Griffin. If irritability had a face, then it would surely be his.

>>How dare you disturb me?<< She murmured looking around. >> The boy there at the fire.. He is important!

He has a deep gash in his leg and its pretty black.

It does not look good please help him!<< Stammered Sven.

The Healer Almina went to Adam and touched him. She could sense his pain, his injury and the venom too. Even she felt unimaginable torture.

Almina reached into the pocket of her robe and pulled out some stones, that she had gotten from her parents.

These stones had been passed down through the generations of her family.

The were black and smooth, but not polished, lay as if meant to be in her hand, and gave off a sort of electric energy.

She lay the stones carefully on Adams injury.

Wheezing Adam tried to get up but fell straight back down and passed out in the sand.

His breathing back to normal.

The healer struggled to stand up straight again and even had to stop for a short moment.

>>Is he going to make it?<< Sven asked cautiously. <<I Don´t know. The venom is very strong and had already spread too much through his body.

I may have just delayed his death, yet my power may not be enough. All you can do now is hope.<<

Sven looked at her worryingly, then leant back down to Emiliana who still lay lifeless on the ground. He covered her, lifting her head gently he tried to get her to take some of the healing Tee.

Coughing loudly her eyes swung open, looking around her in shock for a moment not knowing where they were.

Shouting now: <<Adam!!! Where is Adam?<< Sven gently ushered her back down. >>He is OK, he's sleeping.

Here drink this!<< he said handing her the Tee. Emiliana looked at him in disbelief, then giving in taking the cup to her mouth and enjoying the warmth and comfort of the Tee. >>What happened? Who are you? What where those creatures?<< You know that's an awful lot of questions for someone who was passed out not too long ago.<< said Tinus, as he poured himself a large wine and emptied the glass with one big gulp.

Almina sat beside Tinus. >>You might as well give me some wine too, since you woke me.<< She grabbed the jug out of his hand and filled her cup.

All the while shouting across to Sven: >>You explain it to the girl, I am too tired and exhausted.<< Sven getting agitated now grumbled to himself: >>For that I´m good enough, but its all on me again as soon as I say something wrong.

The old hag bugs me and then goes and drinks the good wine without me! My night couldn't get any better than this...<< He

added sarcastically, still mumbling to himself uttering words that only he could understand. Emiliana in the mean time had crawled her way over to Adam, sobbing quietly, because he wasn't reacting to her at all. Sven sat himself her, throwing extra twigs and wood on the fire, causing embers to fly around. He looked at her then. >> You two
 encountered creatures that aren't from this world. They are creatures of the night.
We do not know from they came, but we do know that they are pure evil and have only one goal: They want to destroy everything! We have been looking for the two that attacked you today for some time.
They attacked our village a few days ago. They killed everything and everyone, even ate them. We drove them here to lake, and… well we couldn't have known, that you were going to be here.<<
Leaving one hand resting on Adam she listened wide eyed.
 Adams chest rising and sinking calming, his eyes flickering occasionally.
>>What about Adam?<< She asked with tears running down her cheeks. >> He was struck by a sword which was laced with poison,even if the victim doesn't drop dead straight away the poison will continue to work its way through the body never leaving.

It will become the victims life companion, and that will probably be what's going to happen to your boyfriend.

We do know some doctors who are already working on a cure, yet so far without results. As yet we have no cure.<< Desperation grew in Emiliana, tears flowing so much that she could barely recognise Adam through them any more.

>>Our Healer here, Almina did what she could to help the boy, but her powers are limited.

Only magic could help him now. We have to wait. Now try and get some sleep.<<

With these words Sven left and went to Tinus and Almina who were speaking quietly among themselves.

Exhaustion getting the better of her it wasnt long before Emiliana drifted off to sleep, as Sven stood "Guard" snoring quietly as he did so and nobody taking notice that a blurry creature was emerging beside him.

It seemed to have the consistency of fog, yet still taking solid form from time to time.

A second creature also emerging now, both making their way over to Adam and Emiliana. The smaller of the two wielding a small silver wand, holding it over Adam.

Fine glowing lines washing over Adam like a rain shower and silently seeping into him.

As the lights dimmed down the two creatures where already beside Amiliana, touching her gently and drawing a symbol on her arm.
No sooner had they appeared, were they already gone again.
>>What happened? Where am I? Emiliana!!!<< Adams eyes eyes opened immediately and he jumped to his feet.
Emiliana awoke from the shock if his yelling, looking at him in amazement and standing now to meet him.
>>You´re alive!<< She fell into his arms and kissed him. >> And why shouldn't I be alive? Look, I feel great! How did we get here ? Am I hurt or why am I wearing this bandage ?<<
Emiliana looked at him lovingly. >> The beasts, don't you remember ?
Sven and Tinus saved us.<< Adam stopped in his tracks, he remembered.
He ripped the bandage off and stared in amazement. >> It doesn't hurt any more, its all gone, there isn't even a scar to be seen!<<
Emiliana stumbled.
How could this be?
Just now realising that they were alone.
Where were the others ?
Even their tracks had disappeared, and the remains of the creatures also gone.
What is going on here?

Undine

Aha ! I knew it ! There he´s already got the next one ! Undine marched to the still glowing fire. >>I knew it ! Yet again he´s gone and got himself tied up with a new girl. While he´s supposed to be mine !<<

Adam looked to Undine confused with a scrunched up face. What did she want ? And what was she even doing here ? >>Undine ! Listen to me ! You need to know !<< Quick as a flash she interupted him >> I dont need to know anything. I know enough. Spare me your lies ! And YOU!<< She said pointing her finger at Emiliana, >> You will not take him from me, that i will make sure of!<<

In that moment Undine pulled out a knife and held it threatingly to Adams face. >> Tie her up ! And then come to me!<< She barked. >> Undine please just listen, you´re wrong, if you...<< Undine livid now waving the knife around staring at Adam. >> Im wrong ? No i most certainly am not, i can see what you´re doing here – with HER !<< She said pointing knowingly at Emiliana. >> But this story will now come to an end! That you didnt want me will now be the death of you! Go! Take your strumpet and then off to the old Müller stables! There no one will ever find you!<<

Why Undine, why are you doing this ? What did we ever do to you ?<< Asked Emiliana with tears in her eyes full of fear.

>>Ask him ! Now go !<< In silence they stumbled toward the woods. >>Undine please let us rest<< said Adam, >>We´ve been walking all day.<< Undine looked at him unfased. >> You want a break? Please! Come here and i will grant you a break!<< She replied making clear that she still had the knife in her hand. >> Then you shall be burried right here infront of your beloved.<< Adam and Emiliana carried on tiresome chained together. The blood already flowing off their hands from the tight shackles that were digging deep into their flesh.

Undine let them rest near a stream after about 2 hours more. The day nearing its end, the hunger and the thirst taking its toll on them. Emiliana greedily drank the water that Adam had offered her. He then quenched hid own thirst before tending to their wounds, cooling them under the water. >> Oh how considerate of you ! I might just throw up.<< Undine teased. >> Go on and build a camp, we´re staying here till morning.<< Adam got up. While Undine tied Emiliana to the nearest tree. >> Why are you doing this? << Croaked Adam. >> Your parents would never have allowed us to be together. You were promised to someone else and i didnt want to ruin your good name.<< Enraged she throw the stick she had in her hands and glared at him. >> You´re really asking what im doing here? Im taking my revenge. The thought of you alone broke my promise of marriage. My future in laws found out about you and threw me out of the house on the day of my nuptuals. A shame upon them. You will pay for this, you will pay for ruining my life!<< Adam looked at her sadness in his eyes, >> I never betrayed your honour, and you know that. I ended everyting as it was what your parents wanted Undine! Many a full moon has passed since then, everything has changed since, this isnt just about us anymore. Beasts are among us, beasts who kill everything and everyone they come across. Many lives are in danger. Even Emiliana and myself where attacked last night. We need to warn the villagers. Please stop your revenge trip!<<

>> I will not grant mercy nor shall i believe your lies. Pff Beasts, dont make me laugh! Your childrens stories do not scare me ! What you are trying to do here is pathetic, my dear Adam. You just want to...<<. At that moment a krusty dirty hand covered Undines mouth, her eyes wide in fear. She was yanked back and no sooner had she hit the ground was she out cold face down in the grass. With the other hand the dark cloaked creature ushered Adam and Emiliana into staying silent.

Close behind them they heard sticks and twigs snapping. They could here the tell tale rubbing of leather and the jingle of metal, then steps and sounds that seemed to grunt. The stench that waved over to them let what little food they had had rise to their throats. Out of the darkness three beasts emerged, their silouettes not even close to being human. The shoulders and arms impossibly big, and as for the heads, they could only have guessed where they were supposed to be. They could only guess as to what sort of creatures were hiding beneath those large hooded capes. It was as though staring into a black hole, with only only two dimly lit eyes staring at them from the darkness. Never had Adam even seen such creatures. Not even the creatures from his scary childrens books had ever made him feel fear on this level. Yet the demons took their retreat, and Adam was glad that he had not yet lit the fire, as he was sure that if he had, they would all be dead now. And where was their mysterious saviour ? No trace was left that he had even been there. Undine had came to in a daze, had watched it all in horror and had not dared to move. Before Adam on the ground was the knife which he promptly put in his trousers, as all Undine could do was look on in horror. >> As you can clearly see, your revenge must cease! We need to stick together. Do you beleive me now, do you see that we are ALL in danger?<<, he asked. Undine held back and looked in the direction that the creatures had disappeared in, reaching for her knife. It was gone! >> I dont understand... What was that?<<, she stammered. >>We dont know exactly, but we do know that we need to warn the villagers, Undine! This is bigger than our problems!<< Undne sank back down, full of shame she looked to them both.

>> Your are right Adam, my hate for you is great, all i had in my heart was revenge and i let it take me over.

With that she untied Emiliana and they began to prepare themselves for the long night ahead. As much as a fire would warm them, they were too afraid to be seen, and let the idea of a fire disappear, since they wanted it to last untill the morning that they would not be surpised again. Emiliana awoke cold and hungry. The air still cold and frost on the leaves. Silently Adam and Undine began to wake. Still half asleep they looked around, got up and straightened their clothes. Emiliana shouted >> We need to get back to the village as quick as possible to warn the people there!<< Adam nodded. >> She´s right, we need to hurry.<< With that the three of them made their way toward the village, still stiff from the cold night on the hard forrest floor.

But they were too late. The sun already high in the sky as they saw the first of the houses. Smoke rising above the village. Undine looked horrified in the dorection of her own house and ran off. The village was in chaos. It smelled of fire and burnt flesh, everywhere lay mutilated bodies. Several houses still engulfed in flames, and many reduced to nothing but embers as soon as the fire had taken all it could from them.

Adam heard Undine yelling: >> Father! Thank heavens you´re alive! What is this, what happened here?<<

Undines father looked at the three of them with red eyes. With tears in his eyes he bagan to tell what had happened. His voice barely audible through the smoke inhalation.

>> Last night a band of demons came into our village. The killed anyone who dared get in their way, taking several villagers them before starting the fire. Only with great difficulty did we mange to stay hidden, and have been trying to extinguish the fires since their departure. Its hopeless. The village is a lost cause.<< Exhausted he took his sleeve and tried to clean his face. >> Where were you?<< He asked. >>And what is the boy doing here? What are doing back with him?<<

At a loss for words, Undine began to try and explain what had happened.

>>He´s alive, thats all that counts. Come on. The survivors are gathering in the Inn. There we will continue to talk.<< Adam didnt even recognise the village anymore. The streets completely covered in ash and rubble. Grey smoke wafted through the streets making hard to breathe. The doors of the houses had literally been ripped off, frame included. There was blood eveywhere. It was the stuff of nightmares. Emiliana took Adams hand with tears streaming down her face. Yet she remained silent . Every stool in the Inn was occupied, but it wasnt as loud as usual. No music to be heard, no ratteling of the dice, no happey yelling after the winning of the card game. Talks took place but only in whispered and hushed tones. Many just looking down to the ground head full of thoughts that they couldnt comprehend, only a few heads turned toward the door as the three of them entered. >> My child!<< Emilianas mother threw herself at her daughter and grabbed on tight. Her father gently stroking her hair. Adam looked around. >> Is that everyone? Is that all the people that made it?<< Marie was stood at the bar, eyes full of tears, she had a bandage on her left arm and her clothers in burn holes. Exhausted she looked at Adam and nodded at Emiliana. He went over to her >> You look bad!<< >> I was lucky, they stormed in just as my father was closing up for the night. He

probably thought it was just some drunken farmers and was getting ready to stand up to them. They pulled him on to the street and slaughtered him like a pig. Mother ran out to help him... Nobody could have stopped it.<< she wimmpered in despair. She found it hard to talk. >> Nobody had ever seen anything like it. Night had turned to day because of the fires that burned so bright and one demon could kill our men. Seven men went to the beast with axes and started hacking it to pieces and two survied the attack, only two survived!<< >>We also encountered a small group of the beasts and had just barely managed to hide ourselves in time. In the morning light we had madeour way to the village to warn you. And after seeing this we can only assume that there are far more of these darkeness covered beasts making their war around these parts.<< Emiliana was now at Adams side leaning on him for support. She looked pale and weak. Marie held up a glass of wine for her to take. >>Drink!<< Emiliana took the cup with thanks. >> You two sit down, i will go and get what´s left of the food, sit!<< Marie disappeared into the kitchen, and reappeared only a few short moments later with bread, bacon and a big pitcher. The three companions sat in silence eating their small meal. Emiliana looked at Adam. He chewed on his bread. Completely lost in his thoughts.

>>What are we going to do now Adam?<< HE wiped the crumbs off the table with his hand. >> I dont rightly know. I Think i will take the inheritance my mother left me. Come with me to my room and i will show you everything.<< Undine cleared her throat. >> I will go with my parents and see what can be salvaged.<< Adam nodded, then thanked Marie with nod and started making his way up the worn down wooden steps to his room.

The wooden floor boards creaked with every step. There was nothing of the chaos to be seen up here. Only the smell of burnt wood hung in the air. His room had remained untouched and lay before him just as he had left it. Adam went to his hiding spot and took out the things he had deposited here. He threw the leather wallet over to Emiliana, who stood with her arms stretched out. >>Look inside!<< Money fell out before her, aswell as deeds and papers of worth, all held together with important seals. Emiliana looked amazed. She ruffeled through the papers with her finger and looked at Adam in disbelief. >>All this belongs to you?<< >>My mother gave it to me as i ran from my father. Look! Theres even a map here.<< Adam unfolded the parchment carefully and straightened it out on the table, as they both leaned over it. Emiliana followed the path he was showing with his finger to the piece of land he now owned. >>Adam i know my way around these parts a little bit, but this place<<, she pointed at the area on the map, >>This place i do not know. And you said something about 30 days ? No Adam never.<< She pointed anew to a different area on the map and said >> To this area here is about 30days. Your destination is much further away. It is far more likely that with a good cart and good horses that you will arrive in three to four months ! This type of map i have not seen in i dont know how long. My parents used to have alot of maps and my great grandmother used to tell us about places that were very far away. All of which i wanted to visit. But i was stuck here after my parents had passed away. The maps however i have never forgotten. Adam that is why i beleive that our journey will be very long.<< He looked at her. >>Does that mean you´re coming with me? What is keeping us here? The people here will flee to the towns and cities out of fear. Barely anyone here will even be able to rebuild this place and even if they were, would it take far too long.<<

He packed everything together and took a little of the money and put into a seperate little leather pouch. Then he looked over to Emiliana. >>So what do you say?<<

>>I have spent my entire life here, i have seen nothing of the world. I am coming with you! But first me have to go to my place, i have

horses there and a cart. And besides i need to
see what is still there.>> Adam didnt hesitate,
went to her and kissed her. >>Come on
then!<< It was much louder downstairs now.
The councel or rather what was left of them
were discussing what was to happen now, how
they would go on. >> We aregoing into the
city, there is nothing left here for us now. We
will not survive the winter like this.<< Said
one of the. To which another replied: >> We
can do this, if we all stick together!<<
Undine came toward the two of them. >>
They´ve been discussing this for the past half
hour now and cannot agree.<< Adam turned
to Undine. >> Here take this.<< He gave her
the leather pouch filled with crowns.
>>Behind the barn you will find my car. Take
it and go with your parents to the city.<<
Undine stared at him in disbelief >> I cannot
accept that.<< >>Why not? Undine please just
look around you!<<
>>My father is far to proud to acceot any help
from you!<< Adam had a crooked grin on his
face >>Then just dont tell him that it´s from
me.<< Undine nodded her thanks and said
her goodbyes, but not without turning to
Adam once more giving him a cheeky wink.
>>Before i forget, you can keep the knife. You
will probably need it.<< With that she took
her parents towards the door and left.

The Oath

The day was almost over as the couple reached the old village blacksmith. The roof sagging to the side as well as the chimney which was also crooked. Many of the bricks loose, with the walls also showing long cracks along the facade. This building that was erected and used over many a generation, almost completely destroyed within a matter of minutes thanks to the demons. Emilianas home was a way outside the main village, yet it was also showing signs of destruction from the horde. Their big footprints still clearly noticeable in the mud. A path of destruction is all that could be seen.

Emiliana rushed inside the already open door, the windows just glassless frames. Everything strewn about the place as if a tornado hit, even the floorboards had been uprooted. What had happened here ? It appeared as if someone had been looking for something. She continued on through the house, along the narrow corridor that separated the house from the shed only through a small wooden door. The smell of blood in her nostrils as she opened the door, there she saw that all the animals had been slaughtered. She rushed to the ladder that led to the hay and climbed it as fas she only could. Adam struggled to keep up with her. Behind the Hay there was a wooden board wall to be seen, that no one would have even noticed so normal it seemed. She moved the false a false wall to the side and slipped into the small room behind it. >> Come on!<< she called to Adam >> Come and take a look at this ! This is where I used to hide as a child, this my own realm. My father built it for me and he even made all the furniture himself.<< The room wasn't very big. Just a few steps in each direction and your head on the cross beams. The walls which were made out of simple wooden boards were covered in cards and pictures of far away lands. Adam had never seen anything like it. Adam turned to Emiliana who was busy pulling up two floorboards pulling out a polished brown box. She placed the box on the too small table, opening it carefully. The box contained many playthings, a doll so old that the face was barely recognisable so faded as it was. Emiliana carefully pulled a document out of a leather folder and pointed to a small speck on it. >> Look, this is our village and if I we use this map as a comparison the place we are looking for should be around about here.<< She traced a line across the map with her finger to the far right hand edge. There she also saw a seal that seemed familiar to her. Adam retrieved his own documents and yes! Both seals were identical. Looking at each other. >>Adam this map is from my great grandmother and as old as this map is it cant be a coincidence that they both bare the same seal. This seal was also stamped on the spine of a book that my great grandmother owned. She always had it with her and never let it out of her sight. I wanted to take a peak once and I got to feel the end of her stick. I only managed one small glance at the book and the symbols inside were new to me. Only the seal was the same as those on these maps.<< Emiliana took a number of things out of the box, among them a small book which leather binding gleamed like you would only know from church prayer books. The edges and spine of the book were warn as it was obviously often used and looked at, but it still held together well. The paper was unusually thick and rough, the sides bound with multicoloured fibres that gleamed. These fibres seemed to give the paper the strength to withstand the time. The cover of the book held the carefully crafted seal. The book seemed to be written in an unrecognisable to her language.

ʌbgd gyculuba dlblb bay gg dbgabz˜bbxcyaʌgduba˙dn rnbgʌ wabaymgba ypd aqbz˜yʌcy cydʌʌcpn dg dyz˜gm rnnnbao ˙gab˙bbnnbgdgcngacu wdda bgcu ypd bcaba cybg cubacynrcpnnnbnno

What was written seemed to be about Healing, Fire embers or Portals. This book seemed to have an unbelievable power over Adam that he could not explain as he was in a sort of trance mesmerized by the teachings. The longer he looked at the words the clearer they became to understand. As if by magic the letters and symbols became clear as day for Adam to read!

>> **Only those who are worthy can read these words and learn from their teachings. Never should this book be used to cause harm to anyone, nor should it be used for personal gain! You may use it to protect your life and soul but but never may it be used to kill!<<**

>> How can you read these words and how can you speak this language ?<< Emiliana asked excited. >>What language ? I didn't say anything ?<< He looked at her in wonderment. Then looked back at the book and everything was clear as day for him to read. The symbols no longer unknown to him.

He shortly explained to Emiliana what had
happened to him and then picked up the
book again, looking at the 1st page and then
he spoke:
>> This is an Oath, to whom the book finds.
Only for good will this knowledge be used and
not to cause any harm. I swear in the name of
my Family Malkier!<<
There was a light emitting from the book, no
more of a glow. This glow came off every
single letter and flowed towards his arms.
There the symbols appeared to collect in one
area on his arm and there they made up the
seal , exactly as it could be seen on the maps
and on the book.
The smell of burnt skin filled the air. Adam
dropped the book. The pain leaving him
gasping for air. Now stretched across the
whole of his forearm down to the back of his
hand was a metallic gleaming imprint with
flags. He picked up the foliate anew and could
feel a new connection with the book. Emiliana
starred at Adam speechless. She slowly

wondered over to him to and carefully touched his arm to check the wound. Then it hit her like a bolt of lightening. Emiliana coughed, eyes bulging out of their sockets. She could sense something, something was there, something she had never realised before. The seal on Adams arm glowing as she felt with a connection with Adam that was stronger than it had ever been before. She could even feel the condition Adam was in, and sense the pain Adam was in, even the fear that had gripped him. It was as if she could see the world through his eyes. In shock she let go of Adam and the glow disappeared. >> Yes, I know, you don't need to say anything.<< Whispered Adam. >> I felt it too! Something bound us together.<<

He looked in the book in disbelief. Again the symbols shifted and changed into a new text.

>> **Learn to use the magic that is within you. It will help you to find your way and with help from your shepherd will you feel your power, to stand against evil. But beware. Only with the shepherd can you learn the magic and master it. Only once you have completed a step of your apprenticeship successfully will the book show you the next step!**<<

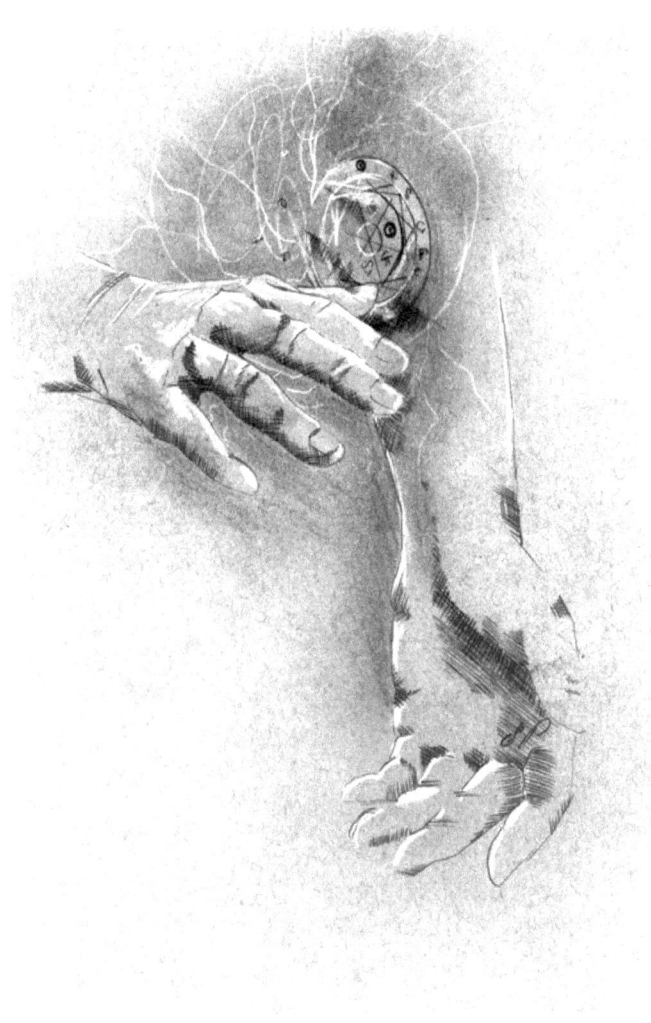

Emiliana looked up and spoke: >> So that was the reason why my house was in such disarray. They were looking for this book! It must be some sort of conjuration for the dark Arts.<< >>No its not!<< Adam scoffed back. >>No its not Emiliana. Its a source of magic, that, I know now. Its a guide to the old powers and energies to be used as they were thousands of years ago.<<

On to new Pastures

Adam gathered everything together in silence
and stowed it all safely in his bag. Emiliana
squeezed through the tiny door and started to
pack everything she would need for the
journey ahead.

It was sheer luck that the wagon was still in
tact and the horses still grazing in the field. In
a hurry the loaded the wagon, and as she had
done many times before Emiliana saw to it the
the horses were secured to the wagon, just a
short time later they looked back for the last
time as they left the property together. The
sun was disappearing on the horizon as Adam
spurred on the horses so as to arrive at the Inn
before nightfall. As they arrived the lights
were still glowing in the windows. Adam
released the horses and took them to the
stables. He threw the stable boy a crown as he
handed the horses over into his care and
called out >> Take good care of these two and
see to it that they are ready to go at
daybreak!<< The stable boy looked over the
crown in hand making sure it was real and
nodded back at Adam. Emiliana was already
waiting for Adam in the bar room. She was
sitting at a small table that was clearly
showing signs of its age. The Beech wood

tabletop showing signs of wear from years of use from the many guests. Rips in the wood and dried in stains adding to the wear. Marie came out of the kitchen with long strides headed over to their table, lit the candle and asked out of pure routine, >>What will it be?<<

>>We would be very grateful should there be anything warm left to eat in the kitchen. You may also bring us some wine. We would also be needing some rations for a few days.<< Marie rubbed her forehead, looking from one to the other and asked >>Are you headed into town?<<

>>No, not into town, but there is nothing to keep us here anymore either.<< Marie nodded sympathetically. >>Did you hurt yourself?<< she asked asked pointedly nodding toward Adams arm on which he had only provisionally wrapped a piece of cloth to cover up the Seal. >> Oh its nothing<< he said with a wink. A short time later they had two bowls of soup and bread on the table. The soup still steaming and the bread giving off a comforting aroma. They hadn't realised how hungry there were until now as they dug into their food, even though the soup was a bit lacking and they had wished for a bit more meat to be in it. Nobody took notice of the two of them as they ate and quietly talked among themselves. The mood in the Inn

seemed tense, the people still under shock. Worried faces sat in front of their mugs, mourning their loved ones and their livelihoods. Adam paid the bill and made his way up to their room with Emiliana. They needed to be well rested for the day ahead and go to sleep early.

It was still very quiet as Adam opened his eyes, the morning still young, Emiliana still sleeping by his side, he was mesmerized by her. Was he doing the right thing? He asked himself.

Emiliana stirred looking at him with sleepy eyes. >>Adam, what's wrong ? I can feel your doubt.<< He took her hands in his and looked her deep in the eyes. >>I just don't want anything to happen to you. You are very important to me!<<

She kissed him gently and shoved him back in a playful manner. >> Then you are just going to have to look after me, that's what men normally tend to do!<< With a smile on her face she sprang out of bed. Adam too jumped to his feet, only to catch her in his arms and kiss her over and over. Just then there was a knock at the door.

>>Your horses are ready Sir.<<

Adam almost fell down down the stairs laden down with all his things, which only led to Emiliana to have a laughing fit. The Inn was still empty, the fire still glowing from the night before with small embers and plumes of smoke spiralling into the air. In the kitchen they could here the clang of pots, there the preparations already being made for the coming day. >> How long would this Inn even still be here if everyone was leaving the village?<< Emiliana wondered sadly. She followed the stable boy to the wagon, who as promised had all their belongings already loaded up that Adam deemed of need, stood out front.

The two horses swishing their long manes around and around to try and shoo away the very many mosquito's that were zooming around them. Impatiently stomping their hooves on the dry summer ground, breaking off small pieces with each stomp so dry it was. The wood of the Wagon creaked as Adam climbed up. He held his hand out to Emiliana to help her up. With a jerk the Wagon set in motion leaving a nothing but a dust trail behind them, that rose in the cold morning air.

Marie looked on in sadness as the Wagon turned the corner and disappeared.

First Attempts

It was already late morning as the two of them decided to stop and rest, the village already left far behind them. Most of the farms they had passes had been abandoned, with only a few chickens flattering about here and there. A dog barked angrily after them, but apart from that they were empty.

They set up at the edge of a field, and led the horse to graze. Emiliana and Adam nibbled on bread and cheese.

Adam lit a small fire so they could drink some Tee, that gave off a wonderful smell of mint and herbs. He picked up the magic book.

>>Look what it says here!<< Emiliana leaned forward to look at the book fully mesmerised. She could only read the text as she touched Adam.

>>**In order to gain access to the Elements, you must learn to understand them, and practice with them. You need to bring peace to your soul, listen deep within yourself, only then will you reach a point where you yourself will be peace in itself . Only once you have achieved this can you try to feel the energy of the Elements. Take them within yourself and work with**

them . For this use the textures that find themselves all around you and use them to your advantage. Only with patience and discipline will you succeed in forming these textures.<<

>>Ok, I can do this!<< Thought Adam as he closed his eyes. His hands touched the ground on which he was sitting. After a short while he noticed a Glimmer, something that seemed very far away and barely reachable. Something inside him told him that this was exactly what he should be grabbing, yet no matter how much tried he tried he could not reach the Glimmer. Beads of sweat starting to form on his forehead so hard he was trying.
Then suddenly just like that he opened his eyes packed the book away and cursed. >> Magic pah! A wonder I,m not laughing!<< Emiliana just stared at him with wide eyes. >>What ?<< Adam growled. Emiliana did not answer him, instead just pointed at the fire. It was still there, even the smallest twigs were already white, and the embers blowing away with every gust of wind. Even the stones that had been placed around the fire had turned to ash. >>How did this happen?<< Croaked Adam.
>>You were concentrating on your training. Then all of a sudden the stones started glowing and but a second later had they

turned to nothing but dust. However you managed to do that...<<

Adam began to think: >>Hmm, what exactly was I doing as this happened ? There was a light, nothing more. I couldnt even reach it, so how was this supposed to work ? Maybe I should try it again ?<<

He sat against the side of the wagon, closed his eyes and imagined water. All around him it began to get darker, until he could see a puddle in his minds eye. Again and again he tried to get closer to the image. Suddenly he felt a strong shove to his side and jolted him. >>Stop it Adam! You're making everything wet!<< Emiliana stood beside him soaked. Where the fire was, was just a muddy puddle and the field before him seemed to have transformed into a small lake. >>Adam what are you doing? Don't you think about what you are doing ? You are supposed to be working with the textures and not throw about yourself with the Elements!<<

Adam just grinned at her, then he lost control of himself and roared with laughter. He kicked something from the mud in Emilianas direction, who angrily came closer to him and shoved him. Both now roaring with laughter slipped on the wet ground and they tumbled to the ground and landed in the mud.

The horses turned their heads towards to humans and must have thought, that they were beyond crazy.

It was almost midday, the sun shinning above them drying their clothes. Emiliana and Adam sitting on the coach man's box steering straight toward a Forest. Both sitting in silence for a long time. Adams thoughts were with what they had just experienced. Just what did Emiliana mean with "Not just the Elements" ?

Emiliana turned to him. >>Well, what do you think I meant ? Do it like it said it the book. See the textures and work with the Elements.<<

>>This whole mind reading thing isn't exactly a win win.<< Grumbled Adam silently to himself. >>Whys that then ?<<, replied Emiliana with a cheeky grin on her face. >> You don't have anything to hide do you ? We are connected to each other and that may be a lot sooner than you had hoped, yet it is what it is. Lets just make the best of it.<<

>> Only what this is supposed accomplish I still don't understand.<< Adam said as he swatted at the horse fly, which didn't want to give way for him. >>Dumb Horses!<< Adam called out as he concentrated on the Insect, that had seemingly stopped mid air in the process. A gentle tingling came across Adams skin, and power arose within him. This time

he could see Emilianas movements clearly ,
but the horse fly still swarmed in front of his
face – as if had been bound mid air still alive.
Not even its wings were moving.

Adam breathed out loudly and tried to relax
himself, and before he knew it the horse fly
flew away, as if it had been untied.

>>Did you see that my love !? I just stopped it
mid air!<<

>> That seems to be the right way. Lets take a
look in the book, because if the task is
completed successfully, there should be a new
section of the book that should appear.<<

As soon as they had reached the Forest the
new book section appeared to them. The
ground darkened from the dense leafage of
the Oaks. The ground rustling beneath the
hooves of the horses as they tread on the
nearly rotten leaves that covered the floor
from the year before. Adam concentrated hard
and got the pile of leaves to float above
Emilianas head. Silently the leaves fell upon
Emiliana. She complained loudly. >> That's so
unfair Adam! Let it be!<< Still laughing he
spurred the horses on to go faster. He had
never seen a Forest like this before. The trees
where humongous and you would probably
need several people just to surround one of
them. The smooth silvery bark had carpets of
moss on it, on which you could see tiny water
droplets. This Forest must be very old. Only

occasionally could you see the sun high above the trees through the branches. It was so quiet in this place that only the sounds of the horses and the wagon could be heard. The path ahead of them was bumpy and all that could be seen was a faint narrow trail left by another travellers wheels. They did not want to over work the horses so they only moved along slowly.

They stopped at a clearing. This seemed a good placed to make camp, and had seemingly also been used by other passing through. They could see the fireplaces and some large stones that had maybe been used as a place to sit off the ground. Yellow mushrooms were growing here and soft high grass that welcomed as a place to rest. Adam tied the horses to a nearby tree and gave them some hay. Emiliana got to work on setting up camp, and gathering wood. While Adam started to work on what was inside himself and began concentrating on the twigs. One after the other they floated towards the stone circle which was to serve as the fireplace. He then sat before it and moments later small flames began to arrise from the small pile of wood.

>>You really do learn quick<<, she praised Adam and pressed a kiss to his lips. Just shortly after that there was a pot hanging over the flames with the dried meat and vegetables

bubbling away inside. The steam spreading the delicious smell around their camp. Adam practically inhaled to food, as hungry as he was.

Just now was he beginning to realise how much the "playing" around with the Magic had taken out of him.

Adam threw another log on the fire after everything they didn't need for the night had been stowed away. He sat beside Emiliana and whispered gently to her >>You go to sleep now, I will take first watch.<< Though reluctant she lay down on the wagon and fell asleep just a few minutes later. Adam could sense how tired she was.

He sat back down by the fire. He was still. A few moths had been attracted by the flames and swiftly had their lives ended with a crackle in the flames. Deep in the forest rustling and cracking sounds could be heard. Adam searched through the trees attentively in all directions, yet he couldn't recognise anything. An Owl flew through the branches of the trees above him and landed nearly silently on a branch close to him. Its eyes where like small glowing embers, glowing orange yellow, blinking at him curiously. The bird pecked at himself a few times with its crooked beak before it then also came to rest. Adam made himself comfortable and took the book to hand. Again a new page revealed itself, the letter arranging themselves so that Adam could start to make out a few words. Suddenly the owl screeched and flew off, spooked Adam let the book fall. A feather floating to the ground landed on the cover of the book. He shook off the idea of being a scaredy cat, picked up the feather to use as a book mark. The text reappearing anew.

>>**Learn to see the things as they really are. Peek behind the curtain. See the life in seemingly lifeless objects and use these like the feather, that you have been given, to store energy. Practice with the feather and then find another object to use to store the energy. Gemstones e.g store a lot of energy. Use them!**<<

The letters disappeared and only symbols remained covering the whole page. He weighed the closed book in his hand again, before returning it to the oil rag, which it was made for to protect it from moisture, and placed it back in his pack. He was so deep in thought that he didn't even notice that Emiliana was awake again and already sitting at his side. With a loving glance he said to her >> You're up far to early. Try and get a bit more sleep.<< She just shook her head. >> Its ok, you go and lay down. I will manage.<< Adam hugged her close and gave her a kiss. They stayed cuddled up like this for a while staring into the fire, that was still burning, casting long dancing shadows over the trees. Small embers floating meters into the air like glow worms, going out as they reached a certain height. Adam could feel Emilianas head growing heavier. She had fallen asleep again after all. He felt so good being with her. As if he had set foot in a whole new world. His own eyelids now growing heavier and even staying closed for a few minutes at a time. Reluctantly he gave up the fight against his own tiredness and fell asleep.

>>I told you that that was a fire, you dummy!<<

>> Yes you did. But whats if its those robbers again?<<

Complaining the voices echoed out of the darkness.

Adam jumped up waking up Emiliana in the process and not too gently at that. She tried to get to her feet. Adam pulled the knife out of the sheath and with a single jump turned to face the two of them.

The two of them made one hell of ruckus, as if ten men where charging towards them.

>>Don't move. And don't come any closer!<<, Adam warned. Yet this this didn't stop the two strangers one bit. >> I'm warning you!<<, Adam almost screaming now.

>>Who dares to threaten us? We are soldiers of the Kingdom of Ellion. No one threatens us!<< called the larger of the two. Now they

were closer and thanks to fire easier to recognise. They both wore hats decorated with feathers and had large swords at their sides. But they hadn't taken them to hand yet. Emiliana seeking protection stood behind Adam. At that moment the two of them were already dangling in the air as if hoisted up by ropes. They instantly fell silent in shock, their eyes growing wider, as the smaller of the two whimpered. >>Mercy! Have Mercy! Please let us live. We are but two soldiers on their way home. Mercy, please Sir Sorcerer!<<

Adam could feel the powers leaving him, and sighed. Emilianas arms supported his weight and in that exact moment the two soldiers fell to the ground with a thud. All you could here was the twigs snapping and breaking beneath them. Wild with rage, cursing the larger of the stormed toward the camp, sword in hand .
The smaller of the two still spitting out bits of grass, got to his feet and dusted of his clothes, before following his partner. He didnt seem as enraged as his companion but still he was to be assumed dangerous with that weapon in his hand. >>Stop and identify yourselves!<< Called Adam. No sooner had he spoken the words had the larger of the two reached the fireplace. He hesitated and lowered his sword. The smaller one came running, screaming and crashed into the bigger one, who cursed as he

turned to him. >>Watch where you're going you idiot!<<

>>Sven ? Tinus? Is that you?<< Tinus turned to face Emiliana, >>Yes, its us, still alive and in one piece!<<

>>What are you doing here?<<

>> We could ask you the same thing!<< Called Sven, still rubbing his chin from crashing into Tinus.

>>We are the kings Scouts in search of Demon packs. Its getting worse and no where is safe from them anymore.<<

>>Come sit with us by the fire, be our guests. We have you to thank that we are even alive!<<

The soldiers sat down. Adam noticed Sven looking at the wine, and threw them both a cup.

>>What brings you to this godforsaken area?<< Tinus asked. Adam sat up straight. >> We are on our way to my mothers farm. We have given up our village so great was the loss thanks to the shadow monsters. No one wanted to stay there any more.<<

>>Yes, we have seem many villages like yours. The King of Ellion has sent thousands of men to fight these creatures, but without success.<< Sven who had the wine in his hands filled up his cup anew and emptied it in one big gulp.

>>Are you supposed to be drinking?<< Said Tinus as he raised his hand and slapped the back of his head, so that the cup fell to the ground. Upset Sven turned to face Tinus.

>>Why are you hitting me? I'm thirsty!<<

>>Then drink water and don't always cloud your senses you idiot!<< He said as he turned to Adam and continued : >> He can drink a whole months worth of wine in one evening if I don't watch him.<<

>>That's just lies! Don't act as if all I do is get drunk!<<

Tinus roared with laughter and slapped his thigh while doing so. Sven turned to Emiliana as if offended and winked.

A smile spread across her face as she walked to the wagon and got out some dried meat and bread for them.

>>Gain your strength some more.<< Sven took the food from her gratefully.

>>So Adam you have learned the art of magic?<<, Asked Sven with a mouth full of food so that as he opened his mouth crumbs flew out. >> Like a pig you eat and drink!<< Adam laughed.

>> That is a very long story and this night is too short to tell it, but yes the power is somewhere within me and I am learning to use and control it<< He replied with pride. Sven just shot him a glance and continued to

chew his dried meat. The topic hung in the air as if it no longer suited him.

>>Where are your horses? Why are you on foot?<< Emiliana asked to break the silence. Visibly annoyed Tinus replied, >> This useless soldier over here had the first watch the other night, yet as I awoke to relieve him he was snoring out cold from the wine. Our horses and packs where only god knows where!<< Sven was ashamed and sank back down into his seat. >>That is why I will take first watch this night!<< Tinus exclaimed ad he looked at Sven still visibly annoyed.

Emiliana layed back down on the wagon and fell asleep straight away. Adam and Sven talked quietly among themselves at the campfire until the tiredness got the better of them too. Adam was already awake early the next morning as the first rays of light fought their way through the trees, to collect fire wood. As he came back to camp he could see Emiliana already preparing breakfast. Sven was still laying against the tree snoring away to himself. Tinus however was already and checking his gear and his sword. Only moments later was the fire going and already had a pot of water boiling for the tea. Tinus trudged over to Sven to wake him with a non too gently shove to the shoulder with the tip of his boot. Sven crumpled together so that wine he was holding rolled to the ground, the bottle empty of-course. >> You really do only drink don't you, you stupid fool!<< Tinus hissed at him.

Sven arose sheepishly and stumbled into the woods to empty his very full bladder. As he returned hos three companions already sitting around the fire eating in silence. Emiliana held out a cup to him that held the welcoming scent of herbal tea. >>Thank you.<< He grumbled with his voice still husky from the night before. Tinus pointed with his cup at Adam and spoke: >>Tell us which path you are going to follow now and maybe we can accompany you for a while.<< Emiliana looked Adam in the face and said gently into his thoughts: >>I think we can trust them, show them.<< Adam nodded without anyone noticing, and pulled out his map before showing Tinus the location of the Farm, to which they were headed. Tinus deep in though studied the map, he then looked at Emiliana and Adam as if he had seen a ghost. >>Where did you get this map?<< Tinus began breathing heavily. >> It reaveals one of the oldest secrets of our time.<< Adam looked at him questioningly. >>I got it from my mother.<<

Sven looked him and now too noticed the Symbol on his arm. He was in shock and turned very pale. >> You two wear the symbol! I knew it!<< He whispered. >> The

place you are looking for is not a farm. It is a Fortress. No one has heard a thing about this Fortress for more than a hundred years. It was said that it had disappeared, as if erased.<<
He took another big sip from the cup and continued: >> There was a time when all those who possessed the art of magic would gather there, and swapped knowledge and capabilities. Your mother of-course was a member of this covenant, but I cannot say if it was as a sorceress or a guardian. But one thing is certain: Who ever wearss the seal and owns the map will achieve great things. So it is written. Let me guess, She<<, he pointed at Emiliana, >> is your Guardian?<<
Adam only nodded silently. Too many thoughts running through his head.
Emiliana too sat before him deep in thought. >> Tinus you said, So it is written. What does that mean?<< She looked at him questioningly. >> You need to know, in Ellion there is a centuries old text that says, that a sorcerer and his protector will defeat the darkness, and see to it that the light returns everywhere.<< Curiously she looked at Adam and asked. >> How far is it to Ellion?<< All four of them sat leaning over the Map with their heads. >> Hm, If we are, << Tinus pointed to the area of the map that showed the forest, >> Then it should be about another 6 days and nights from here to Ellion.<<

>> But Tinus!<< Sven pointed along the route they wanted to take , >> If we want to take this route, remember the Fairyland. I am not keen on the legends about the Fairies at all!<< >> What is it with and fairies huh? No one has seen Fairies in over a hundred years so stop your silly bellyaching. This is the fasted route to Ellion and this is the route we are going to take!<< With these words he rolled up the map and gave it to Adam. The camp was quickly taken down.

The two soldiers took their seats at the back of the wagon and they were on their way. The wheels clattering along through the many holes that were scattered along the hard path. Sven wasnt taking to this unsteady at all. He was pale and pulled a face with every pothole they hit. Only as the sun was low on the horrizon again did the horses stop at the edge of a large clearing.

Elves

Adam secured the horses to a tree, brushed them down and checked their hooves. After he had seen to the horses he sat down to their little group and they ate Bread and Cheese. Sven recovered noticeably. Now leaning against a tree polishing his sword. The cross guard had seen better days by now. Not only was it bent, no, the brass was also showing signs of age and growing darker, and some areas had brass rust as if it had been left to the elements laying on a field somewhere.

Tinus chewed on his piece of Cheese deep in thought, just then an arrow whizzed past him and stuck in the ground right there. With a jolt he was on his feet looking for the direction from where the arrow came. The blade in his hand at ready awaiting his foe. But no one was to be seen. Again another arrow struck in the exact same place the first one had landed. Sven ducked beside Tinus also looking attentively around himself. No one was there. Just then as Sven was about to speak, there stood a large skinny woman beside them. She wore a hunting dress, very long and with a slit all the way up to the hip showing off a slender leg. A Quiver as well as a knife tied to hip held in place with a simple belt. Her light hair waving over her shoulders and bright green eyes scanning the group. It took Sven's breath away. Adam and Emiliana still sitiing on the ground in shock as they looked up to her in awe, just as she was about to speak: >>You are tresspassing on Fairy territory and I sense that at least one you has the gift of sorcery. What are you doing here?<<

The Fairy lowered her bow and Tinus relaxed a little.

>>We are on our way to Ellion.<< Tinus looked straight at her pretty face. >> We do not come with bad ittentions.<<

>>This decision will be brought to our counsel, and the tests will show if you speak the truth and if you will live. Follow me!<< Sven followed her yearningly. As she walked, her long dress revealed her legs with every long stride... He then got suddenly serious. >> Old wives tale indeed!<< He said prodding his forehead with his finger! >> I warned you! An encounter with a fairy means nothing good. But you didn't want to listen!<< Tinus turned to face them. >>Come on! We don't have a choice, we need to follow her.<< Moments later their wagon was being pulled along a narrow path. Trees were blocking their way . Several of the Beech trees where so tall that you could barely see the top, the trunks bigger than anything the group had ever seen.

>>Wait, we cannot continue this way!<<
Adam called out to the Fairy. Still walking she turned at looked at Adam. >> Things aren't always what they appear to be! Continue on through!<<

Adam didn't understand. Emiliana took the reigns from him and didnt hesitate for a second. The horses began moving forward toward the tight line of trees. Suddenly the horses disappeared before their eyes as if cut off, and just after that it went through them all with a tingle and a crackle. Here there were no longer any trees to be seen and they had to shield their eyes with hands so bright was the sun. Just a short distance in front of them was a massive clearing with a lot of buildings. I giant tower could be seen in the distance as if floating. The Fairy folk scurrying through the streets all turning their heads to these visitors curiously. Their whisper quite audible and non to little grabbing for their bows. Their leader however quick to reassure them that they did not pose a threat to them. Sven didn't know where to look. Beautiful tall woman everywhere, each one prettier than the last. The clothing they wore left little to the imagination in his eyes and he allowed himself a closer look at a few of them. Emiliana looked at him and grinned to herself.

Every one of them had only ever heard of these magical creatures in folklore. They drove past lots of houses and even a black smith. A young fairy child hurried after them, as the parents eyes followed worryingly. They came closer and closer to the tower and only now did they see that it wasn't just a tower but a Fortress, that was bound with the Forest that surrounded it. The trees seemingly creating the walls that protected it as if to serve the inhabitants. The path to Fortress was over a large hill. As far as the eye could see there houses and fields filled to the brim. A large river crossed their path and a large bridge led them across straight toward the large gates that had large Fairy like statues standing guard on either side, staring down at them menacingly.

Tinus didn't quite understand just yet what was going on. He couldn't wrap his head around from where all this had appeared from no where. For so many years had he travelled through the great forest in every direction and never had he come across this. >> This Giant Tower<<, He thought, >> It must be visible for miles in every direction.<<, his amazement was halted as he saw that huge statues that stood guarding the gates and the courtyard behind them. The streets where paved perfectly with white brick and looked like they had green and red veins running through them. There was an outdoor staircase in front of them decorated with only the finest of paintings depicting plants and animals, and reached higher than the houses around them. The Fairy gestured for them to wait there, she hurried up the stairs in large strides and disappeared through the door that was heavily guarded on both sides. Adam helped Emiliana down from the wagon and they both now stood in-front of it waiting. Sven was visibly nervous, stepping from side to side, his hand nestled against his sword cord. Tinus getting annoyed now ordered him to just stand still. A small group of Elves came out of the palace and made their way down the steps.

Several of them carrying longbows and other carrying no weapons but dressed very finely. The group was asked to lay down all of their weapons. Tinus made the impression that he would not obey, but Emiliana gently lay a hand on his arm and gave him a nod as if she knew exactly what to do. Tinus gave in and Adam also handed over his blade, and in doing so revealed the seal on his arm for a short moment. One of the Elves eyes widened and he coughed, another started speaking in a language neither of them had ever heard nor understood. One of the other Elves walked over to Adam and starred at him piercingly. His deep blue eyes seemed to be able to look straight into your soul. Adam nearly froze at this. >> You are Malkiers son! Why do you bare the mark of the sorcerers?<< His voice was gentle but still held a tone of authority. >> Who are you ? And what is all this ?<< Adam blurted out as he tried to cover up his arm again.

>> I am Elodiron, King of the Elves, and this here,<<, he said gesturing to the land around him, >> this is my realm. The Elf that led you here, Nalani, has been watching you for a while, we have been waiting for the one that bares the mark for a long time. Yet we did not expect it to be the son of Malkier.<< Adam just stared questioningly back at him. >> What does that have to do with my father?<< >>It is not about your father, but one of his ancestors who nearly managed to once erase our whole race. He was a very powerful sorcerer you must know. Very few people have mastered the art of magic as he did. But one day he learned the nearly forgotten "Book of Elements". We too had only ever heard of it in the tales that had been passed down... let us go inside the palace. We will test you later, but until then there is much to be discussed. Please be our guests!<<

Inside it was comfortably cool. Servers came to them immediately and let them over to a large table.

All sorts of delicious meals and drinks were served as Elodiron began to speak again.
>> As your ancestor found the "Book of Elements" he was obsessed as if possessed and practised every day, over and over the forgotten magic's, he unlocked the magical key and forgot himself and all those around him.<< Adam remembered the not too long ago mumbled words of hid father and shuddered. The King continued. >>Young Sorcerer, what your ancestor did will never be forgiven. Through his studies he awakened forces that even he could not control. In order to possess the old powers of the Elements he needed to pull the energy from the land around him, and as such he used it up with every further spell and every further script, to decipher them. He didn't notice or it didn't interest him that the Fairies around him began to fall ill. His only goal was to decipher the secrets in the Book. As more and more Elves found their deaths with each passing day, the Elven counsel was called upon and the decision was made that this was to stop immediately. They took the "Book of Elements" from the Sorcerer and all of his notes. No one was ever supposed to have access to it again. He was banished from the Elven Realm and the book well hidden. Until now it has never been found. Yet, now you

stand before me and you bare the mark on your arm...<<

Adam felt more uneasy with every sentence. He sought out Emilianas hand and looked at her scepticism.

We too hide ourselves from the world out there after the book was hidden. We have been living cut off from the world for more than one hundred years, and with his we protect the knowledge of such powers. We did however find out that the dark arts had been called upon and indeed used. It was not hard to find you.<<

Adam felt sick. >>What is my task? What does the mark on my arm mean and the map my mother gave me?<<

>>Young sorcerer, before we answer all your questions you must partake in a task, that will show if you are worthy to stand against the dark arts and resist them.<<

Sven shuffled in his chair, turned to the King and asked: >>What is our part in all this?<<

>> You two soldiers will accompany Adam, just as you have been doing thus far. And even his guardian will not leave his side. Only once the test has been successfully completed, will he with the help of the Elf staff be a part of the magic. He will however only know how to use the staff, once he has gathered enough knowledge and this knowledge will be shown by the "Book of Elements".<<

Tinus had not spoken one word since entering the Palace. He could barely believe what he was hearing and after the Kings speech he was fighting to find his words. >>King Elodiron, we are but soldiers and scouts of the Kingdom of Ellion, we are on our way to our realm, to show Adam to our King there. A deferring of this kind is not possible.<< The Elf King looked up. >>Soldier! So it is written and so it shall be done! Adam will be tested and still on this day, and only when he is worthy to carry the Fairy Staff will you be allowed to continue on your journey!<< Tinus opened his eyes appalled >>But, my King, he waits...<< the Elf King called out nearly impossibly loud: >> It will be done as foretold! And even you will wait, until you know the result of the test!<< Sven needed to drink something. Svens eyes were searching the table for wine during their quarrel. He found it, sitting himself beside it he filled his cup to the brim. >>King Elodiron what sort of test will this be? What exactly is expected of me?<<, Adam asked hesitently. The King gestured to mural on the wall, one that stretched the complete length of the hall they were sitting in.

On the mural there was a portal to be recognised, a portal that seemed to have sun rays surrounding it. The mural told a story and showed many a man going through the opening. The other side of the mural however showed mounds of dead bodies with a skull hovering above them. >>Young Sorcerer<<, said the King, >>This portal will test you, and should you be seen to carry the dark arts within you, then you too will not survive the passing through. Should the magic within you be pure, then you will be able to take the Fairy Staff and we will help you. With our help you will be able to use the Staff in the fight against the darkness.<< Adam didn't even remotely understand what was going here. So many things have happened since that night at the lake, and now more tests were being expected of him, tests that might cost him his life. He sensed Emilianas presence as he was trying to grasp what was going on. She silently whispered into his thoughts, >> Adam do not fear yourself. I am with you. Together we will succeed.<< His face began to light up and he gently squeezed her hand. >>King Elodiron,<<, He said with his voice slightly raised, >> I will partake in this test on the condition that no harm will come to my friends!<< With this Nalani stepped forward and spoke. >> It is not your place to be making demands!<< Elodiron interupted the angry Elf Warrior. >>Your will, be done, young Sorcerer. You have my word as King!<< Four guards came out of the backround to the group. They led the group down through the dank cellars of the fortress.

The Test

The cold air in the catacombs smelled mouldy. The stairs were covered in a centimetre thick layer of dust. Its been a long time since anyone has been here. At a large heavy wooden gate there stood two Fairy Warriors who bowed down to their King and stepped aside. The door was locked with four gold plated steel bands. The whole entrance was covered in extravagantly decorated Runes. King Elodiron gestured to Adam that he may step forward. >>Touch it!<< He ordered. Adam carefully reached out his hand, his heart beating so loudly in his chest, that he was certain that everyone in the room could hear it too. Suddenly it struck him like lightning. The symbols on the door began to light up and started shifting their positions just as they had been doing in the Book of Magic. He could read what was written there!

>>**Enter Young Sorcerer, and Succeed**!<<

there was a loud whirring to be heard. With a loud clack the top band was released and swung down. Then it was silent again. Emiliana stepped forward bravely and also reached her hand out to the door. Again the

Runes shifted and began to reveal a new message.

>>Guardian of the knowlede, accompany and protect ! Enter!<<

The second band was released. Now it was Tinus and Svens turn and everything was repeated. Dust and spider webs were swept from the edges of the door, and with a quiet squeak the mossy door swung open. Behind it a large hall appeared and cold air swept out toward them.

Adam stepped through the door and with every step he took Runes glowed before him, that flowed into the middle of the hall and formed a perfect circle there. The hall got brighter with every Rune that glowed. Soon the whole hall was aglow. Just now did they even notice that around the circle stood some overly large statues, as guards looking down on the intruders with serious faces. Svens sheer fear was clearly written on his face as he ducked in behind Tinus without being noticed. Emiliana on the other hand just stood and be-wondered all the splendour that was before her. She had never seen anything like it. As the runes had reached the middle a type of gate arose from the ground, gleaming with gold and covered with pictures and scriptures. There was a black mass of something with the arc of the gate that was as though it was made out of water. Though it shone and reflected Adam who now stood right in front of it.

>>Go now!<< Said King Elodiron. >>Go and return to us!<<

Adam stumbled forward his knees weak. Still holding on to Emilianas hand he could feel her fear and tried to calm her. >>What ever happens, we will find each other again.<< Then he let her go and stepped through the portal. The others saw how it appeared to swallow him and fell silent. Sven snuck silently back towards the entrance. He had every intention of leaving the room. >>Where are you going soldier?<< King Elodiron yelled with a thunderous voice. Sven stopped dead in his tracks, turned to face the King and pushed his knees together. >>Forgive me Sir King, its the wine... I just needed to go...<<

>>Silence, turn around and go back! First complete your task like a man and don't be a coward!<< With his head bowed down Sven returned to Tinus and stood beside him, who just looked at him in disappointment and shook his head. Meanwhile Emiliana had stepped forward through the portal and disappeared silently .

The two soldiers followed her through, even though Tinus had held Sven by the collar and dragged him through behind him. Just like

that the hall went dark and Nalani lit a torch.
>> Father ? How long do you suppose it will be until they return to us?<<
Elodiron turned to face her. >> I can not say. Every one of them must find their place and recognise their strengths and weaknesses. They must each face their foreseen tasks and overcome them. Only once they are truly pure will the portal let them return to our world, otherwise we will never hear from them ever again.

A New World

Adam felt a tingling sensation as he stepped through the gate. For a moment everything went dark around Adam, just as fast Adam found himself on a field. There were only very few clouds in the sky and the sun warmed him. In the distance he could see houses. Adam looked around in awe. Where was Emiliana ? She was supposed to follow him. The birds were chirping among themselves but there was no people to be seen. >>But where am I ?<< Adam thought just as he was starting to feel Emilianas presence. Again he starting looking around but alas still no one to be seen. Then he closed his eyes and searched deep inside himself. She was there, even if it was far away. He opened his eyes and began to walk in the direction that he could sense her in. The path led him directly towards the houses that he had already seen in the distance. Pretty soon he could make out the individual properties. On the nearby fields he could see people hard at work and was surprised. Everything seemed so familiar to him. But no it couldn't be. His village was destroyed. He sped up his pace and shortly later arrived at the town square. Yes, it was actually his home ! >> How did I get here?<< Adam asked himself in shock.

>>Awk look, our Adam!<<, Undines mother called out, she was in the middle of paying her husbands bar tab, who had for sure spent last night drinking far too much. But Maries father was dead? Just what was going on here ? Was he dreaming everything? Marie was already winking at him and gesturing for him to come over to her. What did she want from him?

>>Come, sit !<< She placed a cold beer in-front of him and winked at him again. >>Its nice to see you.<< She gently touched his hand. She looked amazing in that dress that accented her curves nicely and surely turns more than a few heads in the bar. Adam didn't understand what was going on here. He noticed beads of sweat forming on is forehead and thirstily grabbed for his cold beer. He had it emptied in no time and set the mug back down on the table. Just moments later a second was placed in front of him. Adam looked up at Marie with a questioning look on his face. >>I didn't want another beer.<< Marie just looked at him with an enticing grin on her face and replied : >> <just drink it Adam and don't be so modest.<< Her looks awoke feelings in Adam that he could not allow himself to indulge. As she leaned forward toward Adam he had a nice view

down her top, but he looked away embarrassed.

>>Oh wow he is shy now too...<<, Marie turned on her heel and walked into the kitchen. Her mother peered curiously through the half open door. Marie did her rounds and took orders from patrons and pretty soon she put a plate of hot potatoes and a piece of meat on Adams table. >>You look hungry.<< >>Marie! What is going on here? Not long ago everything in the village was destroyed and now its as if nothing ever happened. I do not understand. What is going on here?<< Marie laughed. >>Adam! The two beers where obviously a bit much for you. What on earth are you talking about? Here, eat, before it gets cold. I managed to talk mother into giving you an extra large piece of meat on your plate.<< She sat beside him and gently touched shoulders with him. He could feel the heat coming off her and could smell lavender perfume. Her fingers gently stroking his neck, causing him to gently shudder. Nearly making him speechless. As he turned to her she pressed her lips to his and a wave of excitement came over him. He forgot everything that was going on around him. Just he was about to give in to the temptation, he saw Emilianas face before him and those of the two soldiers, quick as a flash he got up and stepped away from Marie. The table

threatened to turn over as the plate landed on the floor and his beer formed a puddle. All eyes were on them. >>Marie what was that for?<< None of this could be real! Marie scrunched up her face and shouted at him: >> What is wrong with you Adam? Am I not good enough for you?<< Enraged she jumped up from her seat and threw a mug at him from the table beside them. Adam had to duck and mug shattered against the wall. The wine left a big red stain on the wall above the fireplace.

>>That's not it Marie, but your trying is pointless. My heart beats only for Emiliana and no one else. I need to leave here and find her. None of this is real!<< he rushed to the door and stumbled out. He was suddenly surrounded by the cold and could barely see anything. He was laying on cold stone, that much was sure. He carefully used his hands to try and feel anything before him just there in front of him burned the Symbols. Finally he understood: he was back in the cellar of the Fairy Fortress.

Memories

Emiliana stepped through the portal and found herself in her old house. The fire was lit in the kitchen and it smelled of delicious food. The scent was very familiar to her although she hadn't smelled it in a while. The flat looked different. The last time she had been here everything was so chaotic and destroyed. Today though it was if nothing had happened. She suddenly started breathing heavily, through the open window she could see her great grandmother Mandara walking towards the house. Everything within Emiliana seemed in disarray. Where was Adam ? He had stepped through the portal only moments before herself. The front door creaked , an old lady stepped inside and went straight to Emiliana. >>You're here at last!<< she said as she pulled her close for a short hug. After that she turned to the stove to dunk driedd leaves into hot water. She spoke: >> My child, I knew you would return. But our time is borrowed and all you need to know is that you are far more than you might think.<< Emiliana sighed. >>Adam should actually be here. He came through the portal before me.<<

>>Forget the boy!<< Mandara moved with such elegance and poise, that you would normally not expect of her.

>>My girl, forget him.<< She repeated. >> You don't need him, then you have the option to use the knowledge I have left you for yourself.<< Emiliana set her cup of tee down, that she had just been drinking from and looked up amazed.

>>Great Grandmother, I am the guardian so I was told, not the sorceress! Adam is the one who possesses the ability to use the magic and control the elements. Well he is trying to atleast...<<

>>Look here!<< Mandara pointed at Emilianas arm. Here was the seal just as it was on Adams arm only slightly less prominent as it is on his arm.

>>Whoever wears the seal has the ability to practice magic. I myself have found a way to practice magic during my three hundred years of studies, and I can show you how to, too.<< Emiliana looked at her in disbelief. >> Three hundred years? How does that even work?<< Mandara sat down patiently opposite her. >> I am your Great Grandmother. Your parents were murdered by a sorcerer called Malkier. But since you were destined for bigger things, I brought you here to the humans world to teach you everything you needed to know. Your human parents gave you what you

needed and loved you as if you were their own child.<< Emiliana grabbed the sides of the chair she was sitting on. >> The, the people I buried were not my real parents?<< Full of disbelief she looked to her Great Grandmother. She however just looked back at her as if this was the type of conversation you would normally have on a daily basis with your Great Grandchild. Emiliana didn't understand the world any more, too many things were running through her head. Suddenly she had an idea. >>So I am a Elf?<< Mandara nodded. >> Yes, just like I am one too. We two could together master the control of the Elements and make them our own. Like this we could take revenge on those that once nearly destroyed our people!<<

This is not my Great Grandmother thought Emiliana. This woman, who was sitting at the table with her was like a complete stranger. Mandara had always been very loving, always had a smile on her face and beamed with friendliness. That thing that was sitting in front of her was full of bitterness and hate. Emiliana spoke up: >> We cant do that. Even as a duet we wouldn't be any better than that sorcerer. And why should the people from generations later suffer for a crime that they did not commit? That would be unjust! My parents raised me better than that.<<

>>Were you not listening child ? Those were not your parents, they were just a means to an end!<< Mandara replied hastily.

>>I promised Adam that I would remain by his side and thats exactly what I intend to do – as his woman and his guardian of knowledge!<<

Mandara took a small black book out of a drawer and opened it. >>Look here Emiliana! I stole this book from the Sorcerer Malkier. Just look! Here it is written, how to use the power and take all the energy out of the Elements and rule over all!<<

Emiliana was speechless. >> History cannot and should not repeat itself!<< She yelled distraught, ripping the book out of her hands and throwing onto the fire where it caught fire straight away. Mandara shrieked as she too caught fire and went up in flames. Sparks came flying off her and with one last curse spoken she fell to dust. Emiliana stumbled out through the door and ran into... Adam? She was back in the Fairy Palace and he was sitting right there in front of her. Overcome with delight of seeing him again, she threw herself at him and kissed him passionately. She had so much she wanted to say to him but kept it to herself, just as Tinus and Sven also came out of the portal. Their faces covered in dirt, and several areas of their armour covered in blood. Tinus neck and cheek covered in small cuts. Sven looked as though he had moved mountains. He was doubled over hands on his knees as he struggled to catch his breath.

>> What happened to you?<< Tinus looked at Adam still in shock and replied >> Barely had we set foot through the portal had we already been thrown into a fight. Whole hoards of Demons and other such creatures kept coming for us relentlessly. A whole army was there fighting against them and we were right in the middle of it all. There him,<< Tinus gestured toward Sven, who was sprawled out on the cold floor just about ready to breath normal again, >> He is more a soldier than I ever was. He saved

 my life and many many others, he destroyed a sorcerer that was bombarding us with fire balls. You wouldn't believe it but this little wine thief snuck up behind the sorcerer and stole his staff, at the same time beheading him.<< Sven proudly showing off his black sorcerers staff that was covered in Symbols just as it fell to dust before their very eyes. Svens face drained of colour as he stared full of mistrust. >>Magic!<< he shrieked. >>nothing but Magic everywhere. I'm starting to seriously dislike it all. How are we to know what is real and what is not any more? Its enough to drive you crazy!<< Enraged he got to his feet and stomped over to the door they entered the hall in. It was locked tight. Even more mad now he kicked the door with his boot. The door gave in with a creak and light entered the hall, and Nalani and King Elodiron entered. >> I am delighted to see you all alive and well.<< the King called out as he walked over to Adam and placed his hands on his shoulders.

>> You really are worthy of the Elf Staff. Follow me young Sorcerer.<< Adam followed to the King to a niche that no one had seemed to notice until now. Elodiron pointed to a Seal that had been etched into the wall there. >> Touch it!<< He ordered. Adam did as he was told. The whole wall moved with a deafening screech, revealing what appeared to be some sort of Shrine.

There atop a red velvet pillow lay a silver gleaming Staff. The staff was decorated with beautiful blue ornaments and was about as long as Adams forearm. As Adam picked it up it barely had any weight to it at all. The top third of the Staff had a large Sapphire set in it and it gleamed as though it had its own light source. >> This is the Elf Staff. A tool of Magic and unimaginable power. Sorcerers have stored their power and magic within it over thousands of years. Yet only those that bare the seal are able to use it.<<

Awestruck Adam glared at the Staff. >> How do I activate it?<< He looked at Elodiron questioningly. >> That, young Sorcerer only you alone can learn. Only the Guardian and the "Book of Elements" will be able to help you.<<

Adam walked over to Emiliana with the Staff and without fear, together they sat down on a stoop and started looking through the book. And just as before new pages revealed themselves, this time pages that revealed secrets of the Staff. Only the page that revealed the use of the Magic from within the Staff was missing.

The ripped edges were however clearly visible. Sven came toddling over to the two of them on his short legs. He seemed to sense that something was not right. >> Why is it taking so long ? I'm hungry and thirsty. And I nice hot bath wouldn't be bad either! Could you maybe solve your new puzzle tomorrow or maybe even just upstairs?<<

Nalani stepped up to him and to his surprise agreed with him. >> The soldier is right. You have been gone for three moons and we were beginning to think that we would never see you again.<<

>>Three Moons?<< Adam said amazed. >> To me it seemed as though I was only gone for a few hours. How is that possible?<<

The Fairy Warrior simply shrugged her shoulders. >> As you enter the portal the normal rules of time do not apply any more, like this an hour can turn to a week and just like that a half a year.<< With that the all shoved their way down the narrow corridor that led through the Palace and pretty soon they were all sitting at the table again. Adam was visibly disappointed that he did not know how to use the Elf Staff. >>Why does it have to be that page that's missing?<<

Emiliana began to speak: >>King Elodiron, as I was in the other world I met my Great Grandmother. She said she was an Elf. Is this true? And is it also true that I too am a Elf?<< The King looked to Nalani and she nodded strongly.

>>Yes<< He replied. >> It Is true. My sister Dylana was your mother. Mandara took you and hid you with the humans directly after Malkiers attack on the Elves, then she disappeared. Many a long cycle went by without word nor sign of her. Eventually we had to make peace with the idea that maybe she didn't make it to save you. That is why we are extremely happy to see, you, Emiliana here. You will however need to learn a lot of things anew about your family and your people.<<

>> My Great Grandmother held in her hands during my test a book in her hands that lloked

nearly exactly the same as our book of "The Elements". How many of them are there?<<
>>My child we do not know exactly. These books are as old as time. Nearly every Fairy family had one of these books of "The Elements" thousands of years ago. Yet this one here may be one of the last ones that still exists... Young Malkier! Rise and show us what power you have within thee!<< The King waved Adam and Emiliana over. >> Show me the Element Fire!<< Adam reached as he had practised for the magic, and grabbed the flame that appeared within him and directed it towards the three large Candle labras in the centre of the room. The wicks of the candles caught the flames, Adam reached for more magic and the candles melted as if they had turned to water. >> Stop! That is enough. <we can see that you are able to control the Element of Fire.<< Just as he had said that the wax caught fire and Nalani called out. >>What are you doing Adam?!<< Who stilled the flames with a gush of water. All that remained a cloud of water stcam. Then the wind set in and the steam was gone. Elodiron was speechless and Nalani was also at a loss for words. Adam hadn't even realised that the guards had circled around him and had their bows at the ready aimed at him. The King came around >> Unbelievable! You have till now very little knowledge of the Magic, can

barely speak our language, yet you have mastered all four Elements ?

In the last thousand years there have only been but two such powerful sorcerers. Speak ! Who taught you this ?<<

The guards lowered their arrows and Adam breathed a sigh of relief. >> King Elodiron, forgive me I did not mean to threaten you. I do not know how I do it. It is just within me. I think and imagine what I want to do and then it just happens. Sadly not always exactly as I wish... No one has taught me. Only since I have had this on my arm,<< He raised his arm with the magical seal, >> Have I been able to control the Elements at my will.<<

The King thought for a moment and then pointed to Nalani. >>My daughter will be your teacher. My library is yours to use. There you can search for answers, who stole your missing page and where to find it. The wisest of our people will teach you the language of the Fairies and show you how to use the Staff. Even though you cannot use it yet, there are so many things that you need to know about it. And Young Sorcerer, I ask of thee, please do not destroy anything else!<<

Nalani, Emiliana and Adam drove to the library straight after dinner. >>Your two Soldiers also have much to learn and will be practising with our guards, and taught how to fight with swords and use our bows.<< Nalani said as they drove down the street past all the tall houses to the library. A group of Elves bowed down to them as they drove past and then turned off at a large fountain with large statues on it. They came to a halt before a large buidling. The house was made of polished marble. There was large projecting roof under which they had stopped that had large marble pillars on either side which were covered lavishly in symbols that were very similar to those on the Staff. Awestruck they stepped inside. Every step they took was covered in leaf gold and prominent blue symbols were to be seen everywhere. Every nook and cranny of this place was very lavishly and artfully created and decorated. The footsteps of the small group echoed through the large walkways. The corridors decorated will carpets depicting brave warriors in battle with Dragons. Adam could not get enough of what he was seeing. He stopped still at one of the wall carpets, and looked in awe at the man on it which held the Fairy Staff in his hand with great concentration. A white light emitted from the Staff and flowed over the Demons. >> This picture bares witness to a War that took place over a thousand years ago. As you can see Young Sorcerer, the battle against the demons has always been present.<< Adam tor his eyes from the picture and continued on. The came to a massive golden door. The wing opened with a quiet creak and as small creature hurried toward them. >> Good day Mistress. Who have you brought me?<< Norilon bowed down to Nalani, his forehead nearly touching the floor. Emiliana had never seen a dwarf before. Norilon barely reaching her hip, his long white beard was plaited and decorated with pearls. He wore a dark blue robe, that was showing signs of its age with its patches. His glasses with very thick lenses hung at his chest attached to a golden chain around his neck.

>> This is Adam and his guardian of the knowledge Emiliana, daughter of Dylana.<< Norilon also bowed down to the two them and asked them in. the giant room was full of shelves that held a countless number of books and scrolls from floor to ceiling the whole war around. In the middle there were a number of tables that looked very heavy. One of the tables that was laden with parchment and papers had burning candles on it. At the edge of the tables there was a rolled up in a ball sleeping cat. Her fur stained with bald patches. You could definitely see how old she was. Norilon gestured for them to have a seat and poured tea for each of them. With one swoop he cleared the table. He didn't realise the cat was there and she was of course

wooshed away too, she leapt up hissed at him and disappeared behind the shelves.
>>Simple minded animal! She only ever chooses to sleep there where no one expects her to be! But sure, now speak. What leads you to me?<< he asked as he looked at their faces questioningly. >> Our Young Sorcerer here, Adam, has been tested, he passed and as such has received the Elf Staff, however he has yet still a lot to learn, and the most urgent needed knowledge we hope to find here with you. Also we need to find another book of "The Elements", because this one here is missing at least one page.<< Nalani said pointing to the book in Eilianas hands. The old dwarf cramped up and stared at the book. >> For many many years I have not seen such a book! May I see it please? Show it to me!<< His hands shaking with excitement as Emiliana handed him the book. Full of deep respect he opened the book and flicked through the pages. Everything around him seemed forgotten. After a while Adam stirred and began to speak and explained: >> One of the pages is missing, and this is the page that explains how to use the Elf Staff.<< Norilon found it extremely hard to tear his eyes away from the book but alas he peered out over his glasses. >> I do not think that you will find anything about this here in my Library. A book such as this is one of a kind. Every

example that I have ever known about has long been destroyed.<< hesitantly he handed the book back. >> I do however still have a lot of the knowledge you will need, Young Sorcerer. Now you may come here everyday after dawn and continued your quest for knowledge!<<

Norilon got up abruptly. >> Now go. Even I have a lot to be doing and the day is already nearing its end.<< he pointed toward the door and left the three of them standing there as disappeared behind the shelves. The old cat buffed up against Adams leg as he left the room.

New Steps

The sun greats the new day. Full of vigour
Adam pulled back his blanket and stepped to
the window.
On small table nearby stood his breakfast on a
tray. Adam had just about finished eating as
there was a knock at the door.
Emiliana stepped inside and embraced him.
>> Come on lazy bones, we have a lot to
learn!<< In front of the Palace they were
greeted by the usual morning coolness under
a cloudless sky, with barely a breeze to be felt.
A summer day could not begin any better
than this.
Today they had decided to walk to the Library.
Even though it was early there was already a
lot of Elves out and going about their business
just looking up to get a glance at the two
people walking by.
 Adam and Emiliana where amazed at how
beautiful it was here. The dwarf Norilon was
already waiting for them out front nervously
tapping his foot on the floor.
>>Young Sorcerer do not waste my precious
time! Come and begin now!<< This time the
papers were arranged very neatly in a stack on
the table.

A dozen books or so were stacked on the table in such a way that they formed a spiral like a screw.

>>Take a seat! These books here, are for you Young Guardian, and this,<<, he pointed to a small red book, >> This is for you.

<< Adam took the book and opened it. He quickly realised that this was a book on the topic of meditation with the title

 "The path to finding your inner self and middle".

Only once you have mastered what is written in this book may you practice magic in my presence. Enough talk now, get started!<< He was still mumbling quietly to himself as he walked over to the other end of the room, and disappeared behind a small door.

Emiliana looked up from her book and smiled at Adam.

He was learning every day now how to find his inner peace and concentrate, to be able to use his magic in a controlled manor. Emiliana was using her time to learn the language of the fairies. She learned a lot about the history of her people and their way of life. A few days later Norilon came to their table.

 >> Adam, show me what you have learned so far. That shelf over there, its has been in my way for a long time.

Move it over there to the other wall.<< Adam looked at him questioningly. >> I am allowed to use magic here and now ?<<
>>Allowed ? You must!
<< Norilon looked at him expectantly and closed his book. Adam went over to the shelf and closed his eyes.
As everything around Adam fell silent he opened his eyes and silvery glimmering ribbons of magic wound themselves around the wood.
He formed the magic strands into a rope and pulled with all his might.
Slowly, bit by bit he moved the shelf to the spot Norilon had showed him. The old cat shocked from the loudness of it all came running out from behind the shelf.
Adam in turn was shocked by the cat, and the shelf went crashing loudly into another.
All the books on the shelf came crashing down flawlessly as if they were made of water. And the shelf behind threatened to tip over too.
The group was surrounded by a cloud of dust as Norilon came over to Adam coughing.
>>Stop! Just look what you've done !<< Adam looked back at him apologetic. >> Sorry, but there was.. the cat was...<< he stammered.
The face of the librarian ran dark red.
He started yelling before Adam with clenched fists in the air. >>

You are saying the cat is to blame? The poor animal isn't harming anyone!

Your task was clear, and you let yourself get distracted by a harmless cat ?

Go and clean up your mess! By sundown everything will be back as it was!

<< Norilon stormed angrily from the room. >>

Stupid cat!<< Adam was visibly irritated . >>What a mess!<< he thought.

Emiliana was giggling quietly to herself as she came to Adam and hugged him.

Adam calmed momentarily as he enjoyed this moment of closeness.

Then he got to work and started gathering book for book into big piles, to first erect the shelf again.

Adam was carrying another large heap of books to the desk as Emiliana suddenly shrieked aloud.

>>What happened?<< He rushed over to her and could see that she was staring at the wall in front of her. There hung a carpet that looked so old that it would fall to dust at any moment.

The carpet depicted a mountainous land. It was surrounded by old scripture and showed the Elf Staff, and there was a cave marked on it.

The scripture below the picture read:

>>Here in Black Rock, lies hidden what no one must ever find. The seal will be the key.<<

>> That's it! That is what we are looking for my love! That is where we must go!<< Emiliana just nodded. >>Come, we must tell the King right away!<< She held him tight and spoke to him with a serious face: >>Adam wait! I think it would be better if we first clear up this mess here before we go to the King.<< Adam got an idea. He walked silently over to the shelf, searched for the calm and his connection to his powers. >> But you're not supposed to...<< Emiliana looked at him worried, but Adam could not hear her any more. In that moment the shelf was upright again and the books started hovering as if moved by ghosts to their rightful place on said shelf. >> Now, that's that done. So lets go!<< Speechless she followed him. Sven let the door close behind him as he sat down on the made up bed, reaching for the jug of wine he had on the night stand. He was exhausted. Those many hours practising were inhumane and just simply torture to him. For many years now he had served his own Kingdom of Ellion, many years of pain and agony from the countless battles he has been in. He bares many wounds for all to see and his hair had already gotten thinner many years ago. He only had a little tuft left on the back of his

head to show, and the deep lines on his face showing his age. He poured himself another mug of wine and emptied it with one large gulp. >> But this time it Is different, Demons and Elves, and to add to that Magic too – this is getting to be a bit too much for me. If this carries on much longer one day I may simply just fall down!<< As he was still in thought he fell back and began to snore quietly.

Just a few doors over Tinus was sitting at his desk and writing reports for his King. None of this seemed very believable ofcourse , but he just wanted to get it down on paper. He has learned many new things here, to be able to use in his next battle. The Elves weapon techniques alone, were way beyond that of the humans. If he would step before his King with all this and Adam the sorcerer too - the next commando post would be his for sure!

He had dreamed of leading his own troop for years. Yes until now he has received many medals and accommodations but this wasn't his true goal. The fate of the Sorcerer did not really interest him at all, yet he would use him as a means to an end. Only Sven, Sven would remain a simple foot soldier, a brave one at that, Yet his only love his wine and women. Tinus groaned, he needed to make sure that they finally made their way back to Ellion.

Black Rock

Norilon was fidgeting with a patch on his blue robe, he was usually the quiet and calm type. That many people at once in this room was a rare sight. Nearly all the Elven folk had gathered in a half circle around the wall carpet that had revealed itself behind the fallen shelf. They all spoke over one another and you could barely make out what was even being said, the cat thought it best to hide in the farthest corner of the room. Two scholars discussing louder than the rest, clearly trying to figure out what the wall carpet was trying to tell them, the two of them clearly had two very different theories. >>ENOUGH!<< King Elodirons voice echoed thunderously through the room bringing an end to the muddled chatter of those present. >> Enough now! My scouts have informed me that the human villages are being attacked more and more by the Dangan troops. Even the smaller towns are finding it increasingly hard to stand against the enormous groups of shadow beasts. Even we cannot win against demons without the power of the Elf Staff or the Young sorcerer. I will give the travellers ten of my best fighters to accompany them on their way to the cave. So that they may find any clues to the whereabouts of the missing page of the book. I will also be sending troops as well as two consultants to King Aron, as the Kingdom of Ellion must be told what is going on and need to be warned. Young Sorcerer I hope you are ready thanks to your studies, as time is of the essence!<<

After diner it was time. A transporter filled with tents and rations was standing ready in front of the palace. Norilon tried to find a way through the fighters. He was laden with a pile of books that he put on the transport, heaving and sweating he managed to load them on. >>This is for the Sorcerer, then he needn't think that he doesn't need to carry on learning on this trip!<< he said in

in a stern tone. Emiliana nodded at the dwarf, and reassured him that she would support Adam with his tasks. Satisfied with the answer, the dwarf made his way back to his library and sat on one of the old creaky wooden chairs. The soft material covering the chair was made of red damask and was already worn in more than one spot, but Norilon liked this chair. He was enjoying the peace that was now to return to his realm, the cat was already back at his feet making it clear she wanted to be stroked. The baggage train began moving slowly. The sun hadn't reached its peak yet, Sven began to mumble again.

>>Why didn't we take any horses with us? Always with the marching!<<
reluctantly he placed one foot in front of the other. One of the Fairy warriors grimaced at him and said: >> You are a fool! The Kings horses are far to valuable, we would only over work them for this cause. The Gaul's are so worn out they wouldn't have lasted a week, and would have for sure fallen over dead in front o the cart. Be grateful that we at least have the donkeys, otherwise we would need to carry all this ourselves!<< It was very obvious now that Sven was enraged, but he pulled himself together, gulped it down and turned to Emiliana who was walking at Adams side. She had heard everything. She winked at him without anyone noticing and while doing so she gestured to the warrior and tapped her forehead. A crooked grin spread across Svens face. With new motivation he continued to set one leg in front of the other. It was late afternoon before they stopped for the first time at a stream. The trees that grew here gave a pleasant amount of shade and a camp was set up. Sven sat on the edge of one of the carts and searched through the provisions until he found some wine and filled his mug. Tinus´ look spoke volumes. >> Come here now and help set up the camp would you! Make yourself useful and get some firewood you drunkard!<<

Sven nearly chocked on his wine and made tracks toward the stream, even though the others stared at him in misunderstanding. The trees here were a lot bigger and a lot of dry twigs lay strewn about the place, ones that hadn't managed to withstand the last storm. Just as he was about to bend down to pick up another twig he saw something flash not too far away. Curiosity getting the better of him he dropped his already collected wood pile and went to take a closer look. As he climbed the hill he noticed an incredible foul smell, so bad that he had to fight to keep his breakfast in his stomach. Directly in front of him was a bush that held a belt, and the belt held a knife which was reflecting the sunlight causing the flashing. The butt of the knife looked expensive. Sven could see more bodies to the right in the high grass. A swarm of flies rose from them. Sven ran back to the back in utter shock. Adam saw Sven running toward them arms flailing about. He seemed to be shouting but he was still to far awy to hear or make out what he was yelling. But something must have happened because Sven didn't normally move this fast. The Elves stood at the ready before Adam had even realised. Their bows at the ready. Sven and Emiliana jumped up and ran toward Sven. Completely out of breath and in panic he managed to speak : >> You need to see this, come on! Bodies! A whole hill full of bodies! Just over there.<< He hadn't even finished his sentence before he starting back in the direction from which he had just come. Tinus followed sword at the ready. The warriors spread out and secured the area. Still as pale as a ghost Emiliana wiped her face. She too like all the other threw up at the sight of the bodies. Like animals they lay sprawled out on the hill. There must have been more than twenty, men, woman and even children. Several of them had their arms and legs ripped off and other had their heads split open. It really was a gruesome sight. All present remained silent.

 Adam snapped out of the shocked state that even he was in. >> We should bury them properly, the smell would only attract wild animals.<<, several hours later the smell too was covered up with a fresh mound of dirt. They all went back to the camp in silence. The wet ground made it clear that night was near, and all sat together around the fire for along time, all their thoughts with the dead. Emiliana was watching Sven who was playing with something shiny. >> What have you got there?<<

>> Oh this, this was hanging in the bush up there. It was too nice to just leave it hanging there for eternity to rot, and the dead can hardly use it any more. So I just took it with me.<<

Adam was sitting by the fire studying the "Book of Elements" with Emilianas head resting comfortably in his lap, as the first troop got themselves ready to take the first watch for the night. Again he had a new page of the book in front of him. He was reading about protective magic and its uses, but he had to read passage several times before he understood the message fully. It was getting easier and easier for him to grab at the magic and to keep a hold of it. Just like it said in the book he wove the magic and suddenly, as if out of nothing a wall of fog appeared around the camp and slowly began to turn into a wall. The guards on watch who where easily recognisable till now disappeared before his eyes. A loud scream woke everyone from their slumber. Sven ran screaming through the camp. White smoke was rising out in front on his sleeping place. The dagger was emitting a dull white light and with a loud bang it went dark again. All that remained of the dagger was small pile of ash. Sven had a massive burn hole in his pants and you you see the raw flesh of his leg through it. The dagger was laying at his side, and r´he must have rolled onto it in his sleep. Emiliana washed the wound and placed a cold cloth it. With practised hands she bandaged up his leg. >>Thank you.<< Whispered Sven clearly in pain. >> What kind of devils thing was

that? And what kind of fog is that ?<<
An Elf Warrior came running. >> Young
Sorcerer, I cannot find the guards, it is as of
the ground has swallowed them up!<< Adam
had managed to keep the wall up even
through the distraction, he let the fog fall
without even trying. And the two missing
guards instantly appeared again. >> Where
were you ? We turned around and whole
camp had disappeared. Even the bright fire
was not to be seen. It was if we had never even
existed!<< Adam grinned apologetically. >>
Apologies, that was my doing. I did not mean
to scare you.<<
>>Your shield seemed to work well, Young
Sorcerer.<< an Elf called out. >> The same
spell keeps our realm and our Forrest out of
sight.<<
Emiliana nodded at her beloved in
acknowledgement.
>> I am assuming that the dagger was a tool
of the dark arts, that is why your magic
reacted to it. I only hope that we have not
called anyone out with it.<< Adam reinforced
the guards, wove his magic anew and only
several moments later the camp disappeared
behind the wall of fog again. Early next
morning Adam was already sitting hunched
over the book as Tinus came over to the two
of them. >>Sven isn't feeling to well. His
wound has gotten infected.<<

Emiliana ran straight over to him. Sven was sleeping and beads of sweat where forming on his forehead. As Emiliana touched him she got a shock. >> He is burning up!<< Worried she looked at his bandage, which had turned a unhealthy black. Now Adam was leaning over the shoulder as he closed his eyes. He reached for his magic and could see through the bandage. He could see the muscles, tendons and nerves clearly. The wound had spread deep within Svens body. He grabbed at the dark evil- he didn't know how else to describe it – and pulled at it similar to that time he pulled at the shelf in the library.

He gathered all the strands of the dark and pulled them back towards the wound, there he formed it all into a ball and ripped it out of the wound. Something dark fell out of the wound and disappeared steaming into the grass. Sven opened his eyes. >>What is going on? Cant a guy even sleep in peace around here? And why are you all staring at me in horror!<<

Emiliana just hugged him. >> What a miracle, you are feeling better!<< Adam fainted, Tinus caught him and lay him gently to ground. Adams clothes sticking to him soaked in sweat and he was breathing rapidly. >> He took on too much. He must learn how to control the power, otherwise it will kill him.<< One of the Elves explained. The gently lay

Adam on one of the carts, cleared the camp and continued on.

Dark clouds hung in the sky, and a cold strong wind tugged at the clothes of the travellers. Cold and miserable they carried on. It was noon before Adam opened his eyes and wondered why he was laying flat on the back of one of the carts. It took a long time for him to remember what had happened. He got up searching for Emiliana. He saw her on front of the cart beside Sven and she spoke loudly to him >>No, Sven, it is not your fault, really it isn't!Do not place the blame on yourself . Adam will be better very soon, you'll see!<< The soldier just nodded and carried on, with is shoulders sagged. Adam jumped from the cart and ran to them. He spoke to Sven as he lovingly hugged his Emiliana : >> Hey stop with the self blame. The only important thing is that you are feeling better. Sure who else is going to drink all the wine we have with us?<< With a huge grin he slapped the soldier on the shoulder. >> I am famished, when are we going to rest?<< They found a fitting spot beneath two large Elms that stood at the edge of a field. Adam could see that the cereal grain was damn near ripe. He thought about how long they had been going so far. Sven handed him the bread and cheese. He nearly inhaled it all, that is how hungry he was. >> Don't let him take a bite!<< Emiliana called out laughing as she poured everyone some wine and handed out the mugs.

Sven gave his mug back to Emiliana and instead asked for water. Tinus saw this, raised his mug and nodded out of respect. Shortly after they were on their way again, all wrapped up in the heavy coats. The rain pelting at them for what seemed a really long time now. They saw a light in the distance just as it was getting that bad that they could barely set one foot in front of the other. Every one of them had silently hoped to have a roof over their head before nightfall and this thought alone made them all quicken their steps. The silhouette of a small town could be seen, with large gates and high walls around it. They had reached one of the gates just as one of the guards was about to close it. >> Stop, wait! << Adam called out. A small guard stepped out from behind the gate. >> What do you seek here in town at this late hour strangers ? We do not want any strays or thieves here at night! Leave and come back at daybreak!<< At this one of the Elf warriors stepped forward and let the guard look like a dwarf in comparison. His eyes nearly popped out of their sockets . >> You are an Elf, a real Elf!<< he called out in amazement. >> I thought Elves don't exist any more ?<< Adam threw him a coin. >> We are looking for shelter for the night, a warm meal and maybe a hot bath. Let us enter!<<

The guard now completely in awe waved them in >> Go to the pub "The lonely Widow" there you will find suiting accommodation sir!<< He wiped the rain from his face, bowed down to them and then closed the gate behind them with a loud thud. "The Sad Widow" what a great name ! Hopefully the food doesn't taste as depressing! Sven murmured to himself as they marched through the town where almost everyone was already in their beds sleeping. The pub wasn't far from the gate.

The nice facade and three stories made it something special. Above the door was a large wooden sign that read " The Sad Widow" and accompanying it was a picture of a woman who willingly showed off her ample assets. The bar still quite full, there were still many guests inside playing cards, while others tried their luck with a game of dice. It smelled of beer and pipe smoke. Beside a large fire stove the sat a Bard telling stories of far away lands. The young people where listening intently and took no notice of the strangers that had just entered. They only noticed them as the old man stopped talking to take a good look at the Elven folk before him. The group made their way over to a large table beside the oven, which they could all fit around. A clearly overweight middle aged woman with a friendly came out of the kitchen and made her way over to them and... stopped dead in her tracks in front of them and looked at the Elves with scepticism. >> Good evening, ladies and gents! I will be happy to bring you something to eat and to drink, but our cook left early today so I will only be able to bring you leftovers.<<

>> Just bring us what you have, good woman.<< Adam called to her. The waitress took their order and disappeared back into the kitchen. The clacking of the dice continued and the Bard continued on with his story. Now and again he puffed on his pipe and blew little smoke rings into the room. The cosy heat from the fire did them all good, as only few pieces of clothing remained dry from the rain. The warm smell of the mulled wine lifted the mood some. Even Sven was happy as a large pipping hot piece of meat was placed on on the table along with steaming hot potatoes, because it was something different to the usual bread, cheese and dried meat they had. A small dainty woman brought the group some plates and knives and forks, she curtsied shyly and off she went. Emiliana noticed Svens glances in the direction of a small woman.

All the meat and potatoes had been eaten by the time their mugs were filled a second time with the mulled wine. Sven stretched in his chair, rubbed his belly and grunted in happiness. The waitress and the small woman cleared the table and asked if they could serve anything more.

>> We need a place to sleep for the night.<< The waitress thought for a moment. >> We still have two vacant rooms, if that helps. The rest may sleep in the kitchen, there is always a nice warm fire going. I sadly cannot offer any more than that.<< Adam nodded and they discussed the price. Happy the waitress took leave.

>>We will take watch and stay down here. You go up and get some rest.<< One of the Elves offered. Sven got up visibly relived and made his way up the stairs. The ground was covered in a thick red carpet that dimmed their steps, the walls polished to a high standard and on them candle holders, where thick candles glowed and lit the way. Sven took the first room and disappeared into it right away. Emiliana and Adam stepped into the second room. It was very roomy. A large wash table with a big round mirror and a large inviting bed dominated the room. Everything was clean and tidy. The two of them alone for the first time in days. They were barley used to being alone together any more. The water that

the waitress had brought up was still warm and did them the world of good. The large soft bed was a dream to lay on compared the piles of hay they had slept on the past few nights. They looked into each others eyes it was a comforting look, now that they were laying beside one another. Emiliana scooted closer to Adam. She wanted to feel his heartbeat and the warmth of his skin. He kissed her gently. Her body was shaking in excitement. Adam pulled her closer still and they made love deep into the night. They fell asleep somewhere in the early hours with happy smiles on their faces.

There was a loud knock at the door. And even though no one answered Sven stepped inside. >> Young Sorcerer!<< He called. His eyes nearly popping out of his head as he saw Emiliana laying there half naked at Adams side. She tiredly pulled the sheets all the way up under her chin and grinned at him half asleep. >> Young Sorcerer, the Fairies are ready to march and the carts have also been loadcd rcady to go.<<

>> Thank you Sven. We will be down in a minute.<< Adam groaned. With a short nod the soldier took his leave. With the door not even fully closed Adam was already back beside his beloved and kissing her. Emiliana freed herself from his embrace and sat up. Her soft skin seemed to glow. Her naked body

causing Adam to rise. Only as they heard loud voices downstairs and in the hallway did they stop their love games. After a short morning bathroom stop, they made their way downstairs to the main room. The waitress grinned at them knowingly. >> Well someone wanted to make some offspring last night!<< Adam looked away embarrassed. The door to the kitchen was slightly open and Adam caught a glimpse of Sven kissing the small woman from last night. >> He didn't need his bed last night either. I have no idea what she sees in him. Well where the love falls I suppose. I just hope he stands up to his responsibilities!<< she grumbled. Adam payed the bill and asked . >> Do you maybe have any horses to sell?<< >>Go down the street there to the blacksmith, he always has horses to sell, we have no room here for them. Our stables are too small for even our guests where are we supposed to keep a horse too?<< Adam thanked her for the info and turned around to head for the door, he stopped for a second and called over his shoulder: >>Sven, come on now!<< Sven came stumbling out of the kitchen as he was fixing his clothes. The young woman woman stood in the doorway with tears streaming down her face.

The sky began to clear as they made their to the blacksmith. Emiliana had seemed to have gotten even prettier over night or so Adam thought anyway. Just looking at her alone made him extremely happy. The blacksmith was in the middle of shoeing a horse as they got there. The steel letting off little plumes of smoke as it was being fitted. With years of experience he grabbed a the nails and hammered them into the shoe and only took a moment to file away the excess that was to be seen over the edge. Then he finally looked up. >> Yes sir how may I help you?<< >> Horses master. We wish to purchase horses. One for each of us.<< the black smith looked around and did a quick head count. >>Fourteen horses?<< he said in disbelief. >>Where on earth am I supposed to get than many horses so quickly?<< One of the Elves stepped forward : >>Young Sorcerer, it will be enough if just the four of you buy a horse. We can easily keep up with you.<< >>You can, are you sure ?<< Adam asked amazed. >> Yes sir. As sure as my name is Kenlad and as sure as I am the leader of this troop.<< >> Then so it shall be.<< he turned back to the blacksmith. >>You heard, we will take four horses please.<< The master called out to a stable boy and instructed him to get four horses. >> I will take fifteen crowns per horse!<< >> I will give fifteen per horse, and you will add some good gear for the horses on top of that.<< Adam pulled his wallet out of his belt and started to count the coins. The blacksmith took the coins and put them away and he grumbled as he did what Adam instructed. Yet he did not seem to be very happy with the deal. Adams reserves were starting to dwindle and he needed to start dealing sparingly. But with the purchase of the horses they were sure to reach their destination much faster, but they would also need to cut down on their overnighters in the Inns. It was already noon as they had finally made way through the towns gates. The horses were laden with packs, so that the donkey and the carts could stay in the town, and thus they could make headway faster. The Elves really could keep up at the same pace as the horses and showed no signs of tiring. Adam kept turning around more frequently as if he was looking for something. Kenlad came to him. >> Young sorcerer what is it ? You look worried.<< >> I cannot explain it. But I have this feeling as though someone is watching us.<< Kenlad then too began looking around on guard and but then just continued on ahead. Moments later he sent two of his men to scout ahead and keep an eye out for what is ahead of them. As the sun got closer to the horizon Adam decided to get the camp set up. The Fairies secured the area and Sven helped Emiliana get supper prepared. Tinus went with Adam to a nearby piece of grass and tied up the horses to nearby trees. As the two of them came back the camp the fire was already lit and burning brightly. The remaining Elves talked quietly among themselves. Emiliana handed them their food. Suddenly Adam noticed how all the colour drained from her face. She stared into the darkness scared, and stiffened at what she was seeing. The Elven warriors grabbed for their weapons. In the distance they could hear twigs breaking and the horses whinnying. A loud buzzing filled the air and an arrow as large as a man and as strong as an arm came soaring toward Tinus, who could not get out of the way in time as he was frozen in shock. The arrow hit him on the top half of his torso and went all the way through, sticking out of his back. The blood started seeping through his shirt on his chest. The horror was still very visible in his eyes as he collapsed to the ground. Emiliana shrieked in panic. Out of the darkness came the Dangans on creatures similar to horses. The arrows of the Elves soaring through the air and several of them audibly hitting their targets. Adam stared in shock as one of the Dangans already hit with three arrows continued to ride, as if the three arrows in his body hadn't fazed him one bit. The panic now rising in him. He stepped in front of Emiliana as a protective shield, Svens sword shaking at his side. Adam began to search the chaotic noise for his calm and grabbed at his magic and the element of fire. He sucked all the power he could hold up out of himself. Then he opened his eyes and searched for a target. A group of three demons came ever closer to their camp. He let his magic have free reign: Large glowing fire balls came flying out of his hands. They exploded at the Dangans and the first of them fell to dust. The other two paused briefly before they too turned to dust. Adam now acting on instinct fired one fireball after the other. Only after the last Dangan was turned to dust did he cease his magic and collapsed into the arms of his beloved. Sven lay beside the fire, he had been hit and his shoulder was seeping blood. All this had seemed like it was just a dream. He wanted to rush over to Tinus who was laying in the grass over there and not moving, but his legs gave way under him and he fell to the ground. Yet he got to his feet and made his way painstakingly over to Tinus. His eyes were wide open staring blankly into the night sky. Any help here would be too late. Tinus was dead. The group gathered around the fallen soldier. Sven kneeled beside his comrade, the others gave him his last honours. Bitter tears ran down Emilianas cheeks as she held Adams hand desperately seeking comfort. They buried Tinus. Sven was affected the most by the loss. He sat himself down at the grave and just collapsed his eyes shimmering in the light of the fire. Nobody could see his tears. Emiliana gently touched him and stroked his back. Without a word spoken he raised his head and buried it in her shoulder. It wasn't until Adam came to check his wounds that he let go of her. >> Don't do it Sorcerer. The wound shall heal naturally and the scar that remains shall forever remind me of this very day.<< He turned and looked at them both very seriously as he said, >> Never again will I let anyone die. That, I swear on my life!<< The Elven warriors echoed his oath as one, and until day break they took it in turns to sleep and keep watch, as the threat of a repeat attack was not far off. Adam opened his eyes. The camp fire was nearly completely out, only a few small clouds of smoke came from the white pile of ash. Emiliana moved at his side.He lovingly stroked her cheek, gently kissed her and stared deep into her wonderful big green eyes. The first path led them to horses who thankfully still stood unharmed tied to the trees. Something gleamed on a nearby small tree. Adam curiously walked toward it and he saw a belt with a lavish looking dagger sticking out of it. A weapon exactly like this nearly cost Sven his life. >> So this is what led the demons to us!<< Adam thought. He left the dagger where it was and led the horses back to the camp, where everyone was ready to make tracks. This time the Elf troops kept their bows at the ready and quivers remained open for quick access. They needed to be ready for the next attack that could happen at any moment. Sven took one last sad look at the grave and got on his horse. He had Tinus´sword hanging from his saddle. His shoulder was hurting and with every step he bit his teeth together. Yet he stood by his choice to not let Adam heal him. The pain reminded him of his comrade. The rode through the whole day without rest. The horizon showing low clouds that got darker in the distance. They need to find a dry place to make camp. The first gusts of wind brought the rain along, that was now pattering against the hard clay ground, and was already forming small puddles. The horses found it hard to walk on such a ground, so they got off the horses and continued on foot. One of the scouts came running and told of a cave not too far away that seemed safe. Kenlad asked the way to be described to him and ordered the troops to

lead the way. The ground was stonier here and the first signs of the rock could be seen through the thick brush. A rock wall came into view before them, and the rock was smooth and black. Exhausted they reached the cave.

Trunan

Sven tried and tried again to light a torch. Yet he did not succeed, everything here was far too damp to burn. Cursing under his breath he threw the wood into the corner. Then out of nowhere appeared a small white glowing ball, hovering in the air in front of the cave. Adam sent the glowing ball into the dark entrance of the cave. A Dangan came screaming out of the cave toward the group. He collapsed in front of Adam still holding onto his black gleaming sword in his claw like hands. Its blood spreading across the wet ground with its head still spinning in the puddle of blood. The horses spooked at the smell and could barely be tamed. Sven wiped the blade clean on the dregs of the Dangan and then gave Adam and Emiliana a satisfied grin. The Elves nodded in acknowledgement. Just now Adam was beginning to realise that the soldier had saved his life. He thanked his friend sincerely. After they got rid of the body of the beast the entered the cave all soaked of course. The beast must have been waiting here for ages. There were leftover bones strewn everywhere and the fireplace had plenty of burnt wood in it. >>Was it a scout ?

But if it was, what or who was he looking for?<< Adam asked himself.

Later he and the Elves studied the map. Kenlad pointed to an area on the map. >> We should be about here. That means that the cave of black rock isn't very far. I think we should make it there within one or two days, if we make good time and have no more incidents.<< Tired from the previous events they all slept soundly, except for Sven who took first watch. The next morning the group was woken up not to gently with thunder and lightning. It was raining so heavily that a small river had already formed carrying stones with it. It remained dark and the group needed to light a fire to be able to see anything. The horses where getting restless in the back of the cave, their hooves scratching on the hard stone floor. >> We are going to have to wait until the storm is over. It is too dangerous to travel in this with the horses.<< Kenlad said.

>> The Elf is right!<< Sven shouted to be heard over the loud thunder. >> I grew up in the mountains. It is too dangerous to travel in such conditions.<< he stood up and disappeared into the darkness. In his right hand he held one of the Fairies Bows. >> Where are you going ?<< Emiliana called after him worried.

Svens voice echoed out of the darkness >> We need to eat, don't we!<< Just a short time later he returned with a small wild boar. His clothes were soaking wet, a small puddle was building up where he stood from the drops of water that came off his clothes.>> It nearly ran into my shot line by itself<< Sven said amused with himself. With practised hands he prepared the boar and shortly after it hung over the fire. The fire hissed as the fat dripped down. A truly delicious smell spread through the entire cave. Even Emiliana was looking forward to eating something different for a change. The solider let out some grumbles of pure satisfaction as he ate. Taking little sips from his cup on the side he looked very happy indeed. Sven cooked the last of the meat and wrapped it up ready for the journey ahead. They spent the rest of the day in the cave. Adam and Emiliana continued to learn for the book of "The Elements. The Elves saw to their gear making sure it was all okay. Only Sven slept, and a well deserved slumber it was too. He grunted so loud as he slept that one of the Elves threw a small pebble at him out of sheer annoyance. He woke up angry >> What is it ? Why are you throwing dirt at me ?<< His eyes scanning the group. >>Ungrateful pack. To get you food, that Is allowed. But to get some well deserved rest, noooo that's not allowed!<< he snuffed as he turned over again and began to

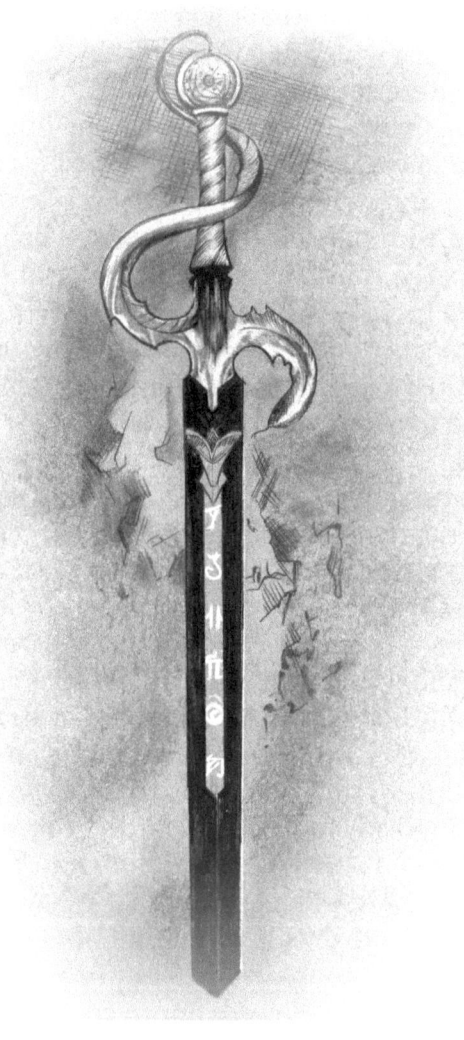

snore again gently. The Elves laughed and continued their chatter. Adam was practising with some black rocks that the cave had in abundance. The black rocks where like glass and just as smooth. Throw them against the wall and they break up into countless little shards, and fly through the air like little razor blades. He grabbed for some magic and concentrated on a pile of rocks nearby. Gently they started moving toward each other until they were touching. He concentrated more and more energy on the rocks until they started to glow. His magic allowed him to look deep within the rocks and could see that they contained ore. He added more rocks to the pile and targeted his search only on the ore. Such a metal as this he had never seen before, yet he instinctively knew that he could work with it. He hadn't noticed that everyone was watching him. It was getting very warm in the cave, as the rocks were emitting unbearable heat. Yet this didn't seem to bother Adam. His attention was on the dark ore alone. He separated more and more from the rocks and formed it into a sword. The handle and hand guard were made of stone that held shimmering pieces of gold. The end of of it formed a snakes head, and the eyes were rubies. Adam used the rest of the gold to make up the symbols and thus the truly unique sword was forged. With a swift flick of his arm the remains of the unused material was brushed aside, and a beautiful Sword remained. It glowed as if it had its own aura. The weapon fell to the ground before Adam with a loud twang. Everyone fell silent, speechless. >> I didn't know you could do anything like this!<< Emiliana called out as she looked at the sword in Awe. Adam grabbed the sword and held it up over his head. In that very second the symbols on his arm and on the sword began to glow in unison. A dull white ray of light came out of the sword and caused a massive crack to form in the wall of the cave. Large boulders fell from the ceiling and everyone tried as best they could to get out of the way to safety. Adam dropped the sword and the light went out right away. Sven came toward him still coughing from the dust. >> Are you trying to kill

us all, Sorcerer?<< he was nearly screamed at him. >> I had no idea that this would happen.<<Adam stammered. Hesitantly he bent down to pick up the blade again. >> Adam NO! Don't do it ! You will bury us all in here!<< Emiliana moved further away from him out of fear. The handle felt warm. The sword looked as though it was made out of black glass and barely had any weight to it. Then the symbols began to glow again and in unison with those on Adams arm. This time though Adam grabbed at his magic and tried to control the power of the sword. Only with great effort was he able to stop the massive surge of power coming from the sword. The symbols stopped glowing and he was able to swing the sword through the air without anything going awry. He tried more and more brazen moves and accidentally hit the wall in doing so. The rock gave way as if it was butter. The Fairies eyes wide open in amazement. >> Never have we ever heard of such a weapon. Why did you forge it?<< Kenlad was visibly surprised. >> I do not know, it was just there. I saw the finished sword in my mind and then just began to form it.<< Sven moved closer again and touched the sword and marvelled at the quality. But then he just shook his head and made his way back over to the fire and sat down as he mumbled : >> Magic, all this magic! Where is it going to lead us...<<

Dwarves

The next morning brought forth light. The rising sun sent rays of warmth into the cave. In good spirits Sven fed the horses enthusiastically, he also saw to breakfast. He had seen Partridge nests not too far from the cave. The birds made one hell of racket as Sven robbed the nests of their eggs. He emerged from the bush with a hat full of eggs and made his way back to the cave. Then he saw her. A small stout figure was looming around the entrance of the cave. Sven grabbed for his sword and creeped closer to the intruder. Out of the corner of his eye he could see that the Elves also had their weapons at the ready and had him in their sights. The dwarf was well built, with a broad back and very muscular arms. His hair was carefully tied with pearls and stones. He had a dangerous looking double sided axe on his back and a dagger on his belt. His eyes looked like glowing beady little stones and his large bulbous nose rounded off the image. His age however was hard to guess. Visibly surprised the dwarf now too had seen the soldier and their eyes met for a moment.
>> What are you doing here at our camp?<<

The dwarf clearly annoyed pointed to the eggs. >> *You* have robbed *me* of *my* breakfast! This here is my hunting ground!<<

The argument brought Adam out of the cave. He pulled his new blade out and the dwarf fell to his knees instantly. He did not dare to look up and spoke with a bowed head: >> You carry the sword Trunan! Greetings Noble Lord and Sorcerer! I am at your service!<< Adam had no idea what was happening. >> Who are you ? And who or what is trunan? Rise and step closer!<< the dwarf got to his feet reluctantly, dusted off his knees and went over to Adam. Emiliana was already at his side, and Sven too had come closer, curiosity getting the better of him.

>> Only a truly powerful sorcerer can wield the Sword of Trunan. It will destroy anyone who had evil in them or is power hungry. However...<< the dwarf rubbed his beard in thought. >> This sword has not excited for thousands of years. How can it be that you are holding it, here, before my very eyes?<<

>> I forged it myself.<< Adam countered casually. The dwarf was now drained of any colour he had in his face, his teeth began to chatter and his eyes nearly popped out of his head. It took some time before he managed to snap himself out of this state. >> You have created a magical sword from the ore that we dwarves have never been able to win? Then

you are far more than just a Sorcerer!<< he breathed heavily. >> And I see you carry the seal! Both of you!". Now the dwarf visibly staggered. Sven went up to him and handed him a cup of spiced wine from the previous evening. Although it had been cold for a long time, it should not miss its effect.

Emiliana now stepped in front of the dwarf without timidity.>>You can see the seal<< Sven took the cup, which had been greedily emptied, from his hand and gave it to her.>>What's your name, dwarf<<

>My name is Brogar. I live here with my clan in the mountains. This here is my hunting ground, but today my hunt has already been plundered<< He pointed at Sven >> By him there. And why should I not be able to see the Seal of the Elements? Everyone can see it<< Adam and Emiliana looked at each other and shook their heads in unison. >>Well until now no one has been able to see Emilianas... Brogar, why don't you join us by the fire and have breakfast with us? We owe you that much.<< With these words Adam grinned at Sven. At the fire Adam introduced each of them to the dwarf and he was amazed when he saw the Elven warriors. When Sven served some roast pork next to the fresh eggs, the dwarf looked visibly excited. He enjoyed the meal and invited

them to join him in the mountains.
>What are you doing in the realm of the dwarves?<<
With a questioning look, Adam looked at Kenlad, who in turn looked at the map and pointed directly at the cave in Black rock.
>>What do you seek there? There are dark creatures there, demons and many other other unknowns! We dwarves avoid that place. They say it is cursed!<<
>>We are looking for a clue to the whereabouts of a page from the book of "The Elements" or we hope even that the page itself could be there.<<
Brogar choked audibly and gasped for breath.>>You speak of the "Book of Elements"? Now I get it. "You and your guardian have been spoken of for generations.<< Kenlad caught the dwarf's attention.>>You know the way to the Black Rock and the cave?<< Brogar just nodded and grabbed another piece of meat. >>It's not far from here, half a day's journey beyond the pass and past the Iron Mountain. On the long side of a mountain lake you will find the cave. But be warned! The area is crawling with Dark creatures and no one who enters the cave comes out again.<< He emptied the cup with the rest of the wine again and turned to Adam.

>>However... you carry the sword Trunan. Though it may not be quite the same, there was a magical soul slumbering within him. This would give you a suitable weapon to stand against the demons, for Trunan was once created by a powerful sorcerer and was always used for good. It is capable of stopping whole hordes of shadowy creatures. However, the sword requires a lot of magical energy. In order to guarantee this, one must form a circle or have a great source of power. If you do not think carefully, the sword will suck all the spirit from your body and you will end up like a dried plum.<< Shocked, Emiliana looked at the sword. >>I understand! The Elf Staff is the key.<<

Together they cleared the camp and left the cave. The day was

still very young. The fresh air and the sun did them good. Brogar led them safely and quickly around the mountain and soon they back on a firm path. Now the journey continued briskly. Their path led them past a small village and many fields until they saw the high dark mountains in the distance. >>Look there! The realm of my clan! Black Rock has been inhabited by dwarves for thousands of years, and just as long we have searched its rock for rare ores and gems.<< It was late in the evening as they reached the caves in the mountain. Brogar advised them to wait outside the entrance as he approached the gate. With a scraping sound a door opened immediately, and the dwarf disappeared inside.

Kenlad and Adam were engrossed in their map when Brogar reappeared. He was no longer alone. A much older dwarf ran after him, accompanied by many others. The Eldest one was ranting and raving. >>Elves, Sorcerers and Trunan! Don't make me laugh! You must have been sleeping behind the rocks again to get out of work, you lazybones! Just a few days ago, you were also...<< The old dwarf stopped abruptly in front of the two men standing bent over the map. They looked up and greeted him friendly. >>My name is Gorm. I am the clan chief in our mountain. My no-good nephew here, Brogar claims you carry the sword Trunan! Is that true?<< Adam turned to the side and showed the dwarf his sword. The whole entourage opened their eyes when they saw the weapon. Silently, the dwarves sank to their knees and lowered their heads. >> He says he forged it himself.<< Brogar whispered softly to Grom. >> Please, stand up!<< Adam called out. Gorm was the first to move and looked at Adam reverently. >> You are a real Sorcerer. What do you hope to find in the realm of the dwarves ? You can not stay here with *them*!<< he pointed scornfully at the Elves. >>For centuries we

dwarves have been at war with them, for once they stole our most precious possession.<< Kenlad looked at the dwarf with a wicked expression. >>We have stolen nothing from you, lying dwarf!<< hissed Kenlad.
>>ENOUGH!<< All eyes now on Adam. >>What happened years ago, I cannot judge. But please be so kind as to show us the way to this cave.<< Adam held the map out to Gorm.
>>Yes, that's where this hypocritical Elf pack belongs!<< nagged Gorm.
Kenlad stepped threateningly towards the dwarf, but Emiliana quickly pushed herself between them.
Her pleading look hit Gorm and he immediately looked at the map again. >> March in that direction and you will come across a lake. >>Here<< Gorm pointed to an area on the map, >>Here is the entrance to the cave. But stay alert! All kinds of dark creatures roam those parts.
Maybe you should send the Elves, it wouldn't be much of a loss, if they...<< Kenlad broke through the barrier formed by Emiliana and Sven. Now the two stood directly opposite each other.
Trembling with rage, the Elf raised his sword. Suddenly the weapon turned into tiny grains of sand.
They trickled to the ground through Kenlad's finger and the Elf looked stunned. His hands

were empty. >>I said that's enough! Your old quarrel is not helping us! And Gorm, that goes for you too!<< Adam reached for trunan. The runes lit up gently. Immediately, the dwarf fell to his knees and all who had watched in silence did the same.

A short time later, the companions made their way to the cave. Riding directly through the many rocks was out of the question.

Sven trotted along beside Kenlad and looked at him worriedly. The Elf had still not got over the fact that Adam had raised his sword to them. The horror was clearly written on his face. Sven pushed his elbow into his ribs.

>>What do you want from me?<< Kenlad growled. He didn't even bother to look at Sven. The soldier stepped in his way.

>>What is this? Do you want to die, man?<<

>>It's just that...<< Sven stepped aside. >>I thought you might need this. It was Tinus' sword. I think it would be in his best interest if you received it and carried on in glory.<<

Touched, the Elf stopped, looked down at Sven and then put his hand on his shoulder.

>> Forgive me my behaviour was disrespectful. To carry this Sword will be my honour! I thank you.<<

Kenlad fastened the sword to his belt and proudly walked forward.

>>Emiliana! Look,<< Adam whispered. The lake could be seen in the distance. Its water

was black as night. The entrance to the cave could be seen on a small hill. Nothing moved. No bird could be seen, let alone heard. It was eerily quiet here.

A shiver ran down Adams spine,Emiliana also looked up at the cave, fearful of more Dangan. Adam gave the signal to stop. The Fairies grabbed their bows and took their positions. Carefully and silently they crept around the lake. Adam's hand gripped the sword Trunan tightly. He tried to be alert and held the magic.

As if from nowhere, a white disc of pure light shot towards one of the Elves. He fell silently into two pieces into the high grass. Blank horror was in the eyes of the Elves. They immediately took cover.

Adam let his energy flow into the sword. The weapon glowed and as in the cave, a glistening beam of light appeared and flew in the direction he had seen the light coming from. Thundering, the rock in front of the cave burst and a figure far taller than an Fairy straightened up. In her hand you could see a long black staff.

Again a white disk of light flew towards the group. This time it hit a rock. The rock literally exploded, so that stones rained down on them.

Adam collected all the magic he could and let

it flow into the sword. He felt the power the weapon demanded of him. When Emiliana touched him, he felt as if more power was flowing towards him. He released the flash of light and it shot towards the dark figure at an incredible speed.

A deafening bang followed by a gigantic flash made the earth shake and at the same moment a shock wave knocked everyone to the ground.

Where the dark magician stood before, a huge crater now gaped. The Elven warriors fought tirelessly against approaching Dangan, while Sven suddenly found himself facing a wolf-like creature almost as large as himself. Red-hot eyes fixed him. He backed away, stumbled over a rocky outcrop and tilted backwards.

In that second the wolf wanted to pounce on the soldier.

Powerless, Sven saw the wolf coming towards him, when he heard Adam whistle loudly and threw Trunan at him. He caught the sword with both hands and stretched it towards the wolf. The blade cut the creature, it disintegrated into dark fog and disappeared. Sven straightened up laboriously and gave Adam back the sword with thanks.

Peace returned.

Two Elves had not survived the fight, Sven only suffered minor injuries from the fall and Adam could only stand on his feet with difficulty. Everywhere lay dead Dangan and her blood hissed on the rocky ground. The stench was unbearable. Adam urged them to hurry, for he did not want to stay in this place any longer than absolutely necessary.

The entrance to the cave had collapsed in places from the explosions. Kenlad went Adam's side.>>This was a dark sorcerer. They despise everything and everyone.<< He bent over something that was in the dust in front of them.

It was a puny remnant of the staff the dark sorcerer had held in his hand, almost arm-length and apparently made of the same material as the Trunan sword.

White runes were embedded on the shaft and a gemstone probably once decorated the staff. A little later Sven found a shiny emerald. It was as big as a hen's egg and the breakage of the dark staff was clearly visible.

Unnoticed, he put the gem into his pocket. The cave was huge.

A hall opened up before them, the end of which could not be seen. Their steps echoed through the silence.

When Adam let two spheres of light rise against the darkness, it took everyone's breath away.

Before them a kind of palace had been carved out of the rock. Artfully decorated columns lined up one after the other and the floor was as smooth as the lake outside. It seemed as if they were standing in the middle of a once magnificent throne room, for far back in the hall was a gigantic-seeming ruler's seat. It was covered all over with golden drawings, in which large black runes were artfully worked in. Everywhere there was rubbish and bones lying around. Cobwebs dangled from the ceiling and it made for a ghostly atmosphere. On the throne cowered a figure, no, a skeleton. His clothes hung down in tatters and a huge spear was stuck in his chest. Judging by its size, this must once have been a dwarf. His skeleton finger pointed to a spot in the hall.

Adam followed the direction and saw a kind of plateau. A huge circle lay before him. Inset there he found the runes that also adorned his arm.

Reluctantly Adam entered the area and everything brightened. Shining symbols loosened themselves from the stone before him and put something new together. More and more signs came towards him and surrounded the structure until finally an almost inconspicuous piece of paper fell to the ground. Adam picked it up and left the circle.

They had found it. Emiliana received the parchment and immediately tried to insert it into the "Book of Elements". No sooner had the parchment been placed in the book than the page fitted in as naturally as if it had never been torn out. Immediately the text revealed itself before them and both read excitedly what was written there.

A multitude of runes materialized at the end of the page.

>>**The staff of the Elves be yours now. Learn the signs and use their power!**<<

They turned towards the exit. Adam looked up and froze. Before them stood several wolves. Slobber dripped from their mouths and their red-hot eyes heralded a bright desire to kill. Each one drew his weapon. Sven went ahead.

One of the wolves lifted his gigantic head, looked in the direction of the soldier and bowed his head. The other animals did the same.

In astonishment, Sven approached the beasts, who then, tucked their tails between their legs, walked backwards and forward. It seemed as if they were afraid of him?

No one understood what was going on here. A light flashed in front of the cave and the wolves instantly turned to ashes. Adam seemed very exhausted now. >>Sven! What was that?

Why did the wolves leave you?<<

The soldier had a hunch. Hesitantly he took the emerald out of his pocket and handed it to Adam. Kenlad rushed up and pointed to the stone. >>This ! This is a stone we Elves are said to have stolen from the dwarves. It is said to have dark powers.

The dwarves found it in the deepest mountain.

Never before had the dwarves dug so deep underground. With the help of this stone they created caves like this one.

Sven, please leave the stone to me and we can create peace between the Elf and dwarf people! We will forever be in your debt.<<

Without hesitation the soldier pressed the stone into the Fairies hand and slapped him on the shoulder laughing. >>With pleasure, old friend!<<

Heavy rain fell on them as they left the cave. They left the dark place as quickly as they could. Out of the corner of his eye, Adam could see something moving behind them.
At first he thought the wind was playing a trick on him, but then he saw more and more often a stocky shadow disappearing behind thick boulders.

Now he saw the buckle of a belt flashing. Only one person he knew wore such a belt.

>>Brogar! Show yourself!<< The dwarf, drenched by the rain, stepped out from behind the rocks. >>Are you spying on us?<<

Brogar looked around. >>Well,<< he stammered uncertainly, >>I have fallen out of favour with my clan because I led the elves to them, and you know how they talk about them!<< Kenlad took a threatening step towards Brogar. The dwarf ducked immediately. He was afraid the Fairy might beat him. But Kenlad just held him by the arm and put the big emerald in his hands. Brogar's eyes nearly popped out of his head and in awe he showed the stone around as if nobody had seen it before. >>You found it! The Shrine of the Dwarves! So the elves didn't steal the stone?<< Kenlad corrected: >>It was Elves who once took the stone illegally, but they were not like us. Dark Elves were banished from our ranks many centuries ago because they had fallen for the dark forces. They have always craved the power of the stone.<<"
>>I followed you and saw you fight,<< Brogar cleared his throat. >>I could not believe that anyone would have the courage to come so close to this evil place...<<
Kenlad grabbed the dwarf by the shoulders and looked at him firmly. >>Come, my friend, let us put an end to the feud between our people!<<

Dwarf Folk

Together with Brogar they stood again before
the great stone gate. When it opened, the
smell of smoke and roasted meat struck them.
Sven sighed snivelling and Emiliana broke out
in laughter.
The travellers were let in and a little later a
narrow passageway lay before them, leading
them deep into the mountain. Crystals were
embedded in the wall at a right distance,
which only emitted a faint glow, but were still
enough to make the path clearly visible. The
Elves had to bend down to avoid hitting their
heads against the ceiling. After a short time a
huge hall opened up in front of them. As far
as the eye could see, illuminated caves had
been dug all around the walls and down here
on the mirror-smooth floor countless dwarves
cavorted. It was like a bunch of ants.
The dwarves suddenly fell silent as they saw
the Elves. A long line of miniature warriors
marched up, their double-sided axes raised
high above their heads, and prepared to
attack.Gorm burst out and shouted
frantically: >>You dare to come here in spite
of your banishment and you have the nerve to
bring the Elves with you?<<

Brogar knelt before his clan chief. >>It is not what you think! You are mistaken! They are not our enemies!<<

>>Silence, stupid Dwarf!<< Gorm interrupted him. >>They may have fooled you, but not me. Arrest them<< he ordered his soldiers. The Dwarves hesitated. Gorm wanted to start raging again, but then he ceased. The green gem floated before his small dark eyes. The lights were reflected in it and threw a green shimmer into the hall. As if enchanted, Gorm reached out his big hand for the stone, but it rose higher and higher and floated towards Adam, who effortlessly fished it from the air. >>Forget your anger, dwarf! Dark forces once stole this stone from you and made it an instrument of evil. These ones here<<, he pointed to the Elves, >>are not to blame. They are more friend than foe! Brogar was the only one who gave us his faith and was not blinded by hatred. He can testify to what happened, because he had the courage to accompany us, even if in secret. That is why I ask of you: Forget your anger and forgive Brogar, for he meant no harm.<< Gorm looked at Adam and the Fairies in disbelief. Turning to Brogar, he stammered in a conciliatory tone, >>Is it as the Sorcerer says?<< The Dwarf just nodded silently and Gorm walked up to the Fairies. >>In the name of my people, I end our enmity here and now. You have proved us wrong and

we are deeply in your debt.<< Kenlad
crouched before the dwarf and reached out
his hand.

Later, they sat all together at a large marble
table, which bent under the abundantly
exposed food. Gorm raised a silver cup.
>>Hurray for Brogar, he has brought us
peace!<<

Sven smelled the cup. >>What a strange
brew!<< he thought to himself. The liquid was
covered with white foam and smelled strange.
But if the dwarves drank the stuff unchecked
and were still alive, it couldn't have been that
bad. He emptied the cup in one go. After
refilling it twice, he turned to Brogar. >>Tell
me, dwarf, what is this brew?<<

>>"Beer" we call it. It's made from barley and
hops and we've been brewing it together for
many decades. Some people say it has magical
powers, but I think the only magical power is
to give you a headache the next morning.<<
Laughing, he lifted his cup and toasted with
Sven.

 Late into the night they all sat and told each
other their most adventurous stories. Sven
was already lying on the table, snoring quietly,
his cup tipped over in front of him.

The first thing Sven saw the following
morning was the glaring brightness in his
room. >>In his room?<< He narrowed his eyes
and looked around in disbelief. He was lying

164

in a bed with bright white sheets and... He was naked!

>>Oh, what have I done?<< he muttered. Something was stirring beside him. A little hand came out from under the covers and a dwarf was peeking out. Her big red curls framed her face and she had a huge bulbous nose. The thick wart on her chin could not be missed. Like him, she had nothing on. She stretched and looked at him.

With one leap Sven took flight and stormed out of the room. He almost fell over the railing into the depths.

Curiously, the other dwarves, who were standing in the corridor, looked at him and laughed resoundingly. He looked down at himself and only now had he realized that he had fled stark naked. With a bright red face he crept back into the room.

>>Hey, what's going on? You weren't so shy tonight!<< She pushed the sheet aside. Feverishly Sven gathered up his things, jumped into his pants and ran again.

What was too much was too much! >>What happened yesterday?<< he asked himself in panic as he stumbled down the stairs. With every single jump from the stairs it seemed as if his head was about to burst. He tried to suppress the dizziness and the upcoming retching sensation.

At the bottom he met Kenlad. >>Sven, what's wrong? Where's your wife?<<

>>My what?!<< Sven threatened to faint on the spot.

>>Well, I'm talking about Enga, the daughter of Murin. Only yesterday you asked for her hand in all that pomposity. The marriage was performed at your request, immediately, as is the custom among the dwarfish people. Don't you remember?<< Kenlad smirked.

Sven had a feeling he was sinking into the ground. A sudden dizziness seized him, his stomach turned and he threw up right in front of Kenlad's boots. He was now shaking with laughter. >>So is the newlywed getting cold feet or what?<<

Sven collapsed and whimpered. >>Away! I have to get away from here! Please help me! How could this happen? It's all that stupid beer's fault, I couldn't think straight! The marriage must be annulled!<<

Gorm walked up to him with a big smile. >>Congratulations, my son! And I thought the Enga would never get a man again.<<

>>But Chief! Listen to me. I was intoxicated by that beer. The Marriage isn't legal.<< Sven yelled.

>>How do you think I married my wife? A wedding without beer is unimaginable for us dwarves!<< Gorm laughed so hard as he turned around and left Sven.

Grinningly, Kenlad spoke up >>You fought bravely against monsters, so will you live through this adventure here!<< Sven shook his head in panic. >>I must find Adam! We have to get out of here now!<<

Behind him, dressed only in sheets, Enga came running. >>Dearest, where are you? It is our tradition for newlyweds to stay in their room for three days and...<< She shamelessly hinted at what she meant by that. Sven swallowed the lump in his throat and ran as fast as his short legs would carry him and shouted >>AAADAAM! Help me!<<

Enga's expression now boded no good and she pursued the fleeing soldier, scolding him. She wanted her husband!

Laughter ran through the ranks of the dwarves and Fairies. Awakened by the screams, Adam stepped out of his room. As if out of his mind, Sven came running directly towards him and shook him so much that Adam threatened to lose his balance. >>Sven, calm down! What's wrong?<<

>>What's wrong?<< he shouted frantically. >>Our supposed friends sold me to some dwarf witch! Help me escape! I beg you, Adam! Please!<< he begged tearfully and turned around to see if Enga was already in the immediate vicinity. Now Emiliana also appeared in the doorway to see what had happened.

Enga already came sweeping up the stairs and grabbed Sven with both hands. >>You're coming back with me or I'll break every bone in your body,<< she hissed angrily. Sven squealed in fear and looked pleadingly at Emiliana. >>Stop!<< she shouted to Enga. >>What has our soldier done?<<

She was furious and said to Emiliana, >>He married me! He begged on his knees and I let him soften me up, because look at him: Small as he is, he could easily pass for a dwarf! And he's good in bed, too.<< Sven turned bright red. >>Enga, first show me if it is written like this, then I will stand by you and rejoice with you. But until then Sven will remain at our service.<<

Sven was relieved and hissed spitefully: >>Surely the stupid sheep can't even read!<< He saw the hand coming, which brutally clapped him in the face. >>Ouch, damn it!<< He ducked to avoid another blow. >>Sheep, my ass! Yes, I can read! Wait, my dear, I'll teach you! From now on, everything will be different for you, I promise!<< Stamping her foot, she turned around and left the three of them without another word.

>>Sven, what have you done? We don't have time for this!<< Adam looked at him reproachfully. >>Forgive me, Sorcerer! I was drunk and didn't know what was happening to me.<< Now he was whimpering again.

>>What have I done...?<< Emiliana took him by the shoulder, pulled him into the room and put him on a chair. Sven gratefully took the cold water she handed him and drank in big sips.

Only a little later Enga returned with Gorm and three other dwarves in tow. Furiously she threw a roll of paper in front of Sven's feet. >>Read it yourself,<< she ordered abruptly. Adam bent over the paper, rolled it out and studied the document. The writing was not unlike that of the Elves, so it was no problem for Adam to put the sentences together in a meaningful way. Immediately his face brightened up as he skimmed over the passage that was pretty much at the end. He winked encouragingly at Sven, strolled leisurely to his things, pulled 20 gold coins from his wallet and handed them to Sven. He looked at him in complete bewilderment. >>Now what? Is there a dowry now too, or what?<< Sven thought he had lost everything, but Adam said: >>Give her the money and you're free!<<

He walked up to the dwarf, uncertain. >>Here... Take it.<< All the color disappeared from her face. >>I don't want it!<< she cried as if she had gone mad. >>I want my husband!<<

With the paper in his hand Adam stepped to Gorm's side. >>Look here, it says: If a sum of at least 20 gold coins is paid within 3 days, the marriage can be annulled.<< Enga's face turned pale.

>>Right you are, Sorcerer. Enga, you will have to come to terms with this. You have taken the gold, now release him.<<

Enga shook with rage all over her body. Then she gave a growl and stomped back into her room.

Sven fell into the armchair and exhaled with relief. >>Adam, Emiliana. I solemnly swear that I'll never be this drunk again!<<

>>Don't make promises you cant keep, soldier, because next time we might not be able to help you,<< Emiliana replied.

Adam broke the silence. >>We have wasted enough time. People are dying while we solve marital problems here. We are leaving!<< She started to pack her things.

It had stopped raining. The sun was greeting the travellers with its warm rays. Painfully blinded by the light Sven squeezed his eyes shut.

Return to the Fairies

Their journey back to the Elven forest went without any noteworthy events and so Adam had a lot of time to learn. His skills in dealing with the power became better and better. More and more quickly he managed to complete the tasks as prescribed by the "Book of Elements". Meanwhile Kenlad teased Sven from time to time with a proposal of marriage, which was always rewarded with much laughter. But soon they passed farms that had been completely destroyed. Seemingly everything had been burned down to the foundation walls and everywhere dead cattle lay on the pastures. They were truly horrible sights. Then they hurried the horses once more and tried to reach their destination even faster. Two days later they arrived in the town where they had spent the night. The gates of the city were firmly locked and on the walls there were astonishingly many guards this time. Adam asked to be admitted. A small flap opened and a soldier looked at him questioningly. >>Who are you and what do you want?<< >>We are travelers and we want a roof over our heads at night.<<
Now they saw the soldiers, attracted by the noise, positioned themselves on the wall and

turned their bows towards Adam and his companions. >>So let us enter. We are tired and we mean you no harm,<< Emiliana reassured them gently. He hesitated. >>Wait! I'll get the Commander!<< A felt eternity later a side gate opened and an officer approached the group. Kenlad was now getting aggitated. Angrily, he stepped forward. >>Do we look like the homeless?<< The officer checked them out thoroughly and then nodded. >>I would say yes. You do look like you're used to sleeping in the dirt.<< Adam tried to be more forgiving. >>A few days ago we were here, and stayed at the Sad Widow's. Ask the landlady. She will confirm it. We'll be leaving again tomorrow.<< One of the Elf warriors approached the officer. >>You see who and what we are. So give way!<<

From the wall, a guard suddenly shouted, >>Captain, listen! I know these people, let them in! I can vouch for them.<<

The captain looked once more at the Fairies, inspecting their weapons. Then he stepped aside and let them enter through the small gate. >>But don't give me any trouble!<<

The soldier who had just stood on the wall came to Adam and greeted him joyfully. He must have been hoping to get a big tip again. >>Where are the rest of your people?<< Kenlad looked at the soldier grimly. >>Fallen in battle agaisnt the demons.<<

The soldier turned pale. <<Two days ago, dark beings tried to enter our town. Seven guards were mowed off the wall by them. Since then, we've been more careful to check who stands at the entrance. After dark until dawn, the gates will now remain closed no exceptions!<<
Adam shoved a thaler in his hand and they headed for the inn. The city seemed to be deserted, although it was still daylight. Very few people were on the streets. Even the shops were not open and most of the shutters remained closed. Even the inn was almost empty. The few guests turned anxiously towards the door when they entered. Soft whispering could be heard. They walked back towards the large table by the stove.
The little blonde waitress happily came running, greeted Sven with a big hug and asked what she could bring them.
>>Just give us some wine and afterwards we'd like a hot bath and a room for the night.<<
Sven ordered a water. The waitress nodded friendly and quickly came back to the table with a handful of cups and wine.
A little later Adam enjoyed the comforting warmth of the water on his skin. The bath woke up all his spirits. Emiliana stepped up to the tub and flicked the foam into his face with her fingers. Adam responded with a gush of water. When Emiliana wanted to do the same, he pulled her fully clothed into the tub. Water

spilled onto the floorboards, but they didn't care. They remained absorbed in their kiss. Only two days later the group entered the magical place where the Elf people were hiding. Everybody there seemed to be doing something and they were hardly noticed. Only Norilon stood with his cat on the huge staircase portal and was happy to see them again. Nalani joined the librarian and waved at the troop as well. Emiliana felt as if she was finally home again. Now they all sat at the big table in the palace and talked excitedly. It was deep into the night when they had finally told everything that had happened to them on their journey. Full of astonishment, King Elodiron shouted several times: >>Surely this would make any bard green with envy, with what you have experienced!<<
>>Unfortunately, these are not stories, my king.<< Adam looked at him earnestly.
>>Forgive me, young Sorcerer. I got carried away.<< Sven cleared his throat and dared to speak. >>King Elodiron, before we started our journey, you promised the now dead Tinus to contact our king. What is there to say?<<
The Elf king leaned forward. >>Brave soldier, I have sent my scouts to Ellion, but they have not returned yet. We must wait patiently. But for you, Sven, I am very sorry for the loss of your friend.<< Now they were all silent and awaited the things that might come.

Ellion

The following morning a messenger finally arrived from Ellion. Adam was absorbed in his book and practicing magic when a rider raced into the castle courtyard. He stopped in front of the big stairs and rushed up the steps with his last ounce of strength.

>>I must see the king!<< Though he was surely infinitely tired, he still managed to summon up the strength to alert the guards. They led him into the throne room. King Elodiron was in the process of convincing the council that the first priority was to join the humans in their fight against the demons. A fierce discussion was underway, but with the appearance of the messenger, the hall fell silent. Everyone looked to the door.

The young Elf was skinny and his clothes were covered with black encrusted bloodstains.

>>My king, I rode as fast as I could.<<

The king rose and hurried towards the messenger. >>Speak, what have you to report?<<

>>My king, our journey to Ellion went swiftly and nowhere were we held up. Then, at the gates of the city we became aware of a force made up entirely of demons. They tried to enter the city with unbridled force. Our

soldiers tried to help the people of Ellion. They sent me back to report to you!<<

King Elodiron listened. >>How many demons are we talking about?<<

>>I mean that there are about 12,000 men,<< the Elf stammered. Voices were raised in the hall. >>You see? That's why we must help. Once the demons are done with the humans, they will come for us.<< Many on the council nodded.

>>Soldier!<< King Elodiron looked at the messenger again. >>Soldier, have you made contact with Ellion's King Aron?<<

The messenger raised his shoulder. >>Forgive me, my king, but there was no getting through. There were simply too many of them.<<

Turning to the council again, the Elfen King said, >>I mean, it is of the utmost importance that we help the people! I will send eight hundred of our best fighters to save the city. Ellion must remain a safe place for its people.<<

Again there was loud murmuring.

Then an old elf rose up. >>So be it, King Elodiron, we send our troops to save the people. I hope the young Sorcerer Adam has progressed and can help our warriors.<<

The next morning, no one stood still in the Elf forest. They sensed something big was about to happen.

Adam sat on the steps of the library and, lost in thought, stroked the cat which, for lack of a name, he had unceremoniously christened Edgar.

Sven hurried to him and gasped heavily as he reached Adam. >>Go ahead, Sorcerer! It's time to go home!<< Puzzled, he looked up.

>>Home? Back to our village?<< >>Fool!<< Sven snorted. >>Ellion is home, my home!<< Adam understood and his face brightened. He quickly got up and ran to Emiliana to tell her the news. Edgar, who felt disturbed in his right to be stroked again, ran back to the library, insulted.

A short time later all were gathered in front of the palace.

Adam and Emiliana looked at the troops of the Elves in awe and the troop that belonged to them.

King Elodiron wished them luck for the journey. Nalani joined Emiliana and presented her with a beautifully decorated dagger.

>>Take this one, Elf girl! May the gun protect you in all your ways. Come well soon!<< Then the troop started to move.

Such a force always accompanied a large group of diligent craftsmen, of course, who made sure that everything could be repaired or even replaced on the long journey - from horseshoes to tarpaulins that had to be mended and completely independent of the cooks, stable boys and healers. It was as if a small town was wandering around.

The road to Ellion led across flat land. As far as the eye could see, there were no hills or mountains to be seen. Just grass and trees everywhere you looked.

Adam hardly let a minute go by without learning. He was aware of the difficult task he had been given. The book still showed him so many possibilities, only sometimes it was very difficult to understand everything at first go. In the evening, when they rested, he sat by the fire with Emiliana and was still studying in the book. This time, with the help of magic, a hole opened up in the air for a few moments, its edge flickering and glowing slowly. Inside the hole was a small marketplace.

People were busily walking around. Emiliana recognized immediately that Adam had summoned her village here and opened her eyes in amazement. >>How did you do that, my love?<< she shouted loudly, and just at that moment silvery sparks fell from the air and the picture was extinguished.

>>How did you do that, Adam?<< she asked again, this time with more emphasis in her voice. He just shrugged his shoulders and looked at her. >>I don't know exactly. But I

find it very difficult to weave this kind of magic. I must try again!<<

This time the peephole in the air got a little bigger and Emiliana immediately recognized the lake where they had met before their adventure began. >>Look, the lake! Are these your memories?<<

Sven, meanwhile, watched the spectacle silently, jumped up, picked up a stone and threw it through the hole. With a loud clap, the stone hit the water. Everyone looked at each other in complete amazement. How was that possible?

Adam also let this hole close and wove another, even bigger one.

This time he stood up, stepped carefully through it and disappeared into the darkness. A few moments later he stepped back to the fire with the hissing Edgar, the cat from the library.

The poor animal seemed completely disturbed.

>>That would be a great way to travel,<< Sven mused astonished and everyone nodded thoughtfully.

Adam brought the cat back. It was only after the hole had gone dark that he realized how hungry he was. The magic required a lot of strength.

For a long time they talked and thought of things that might be possible with magic. A gateway for travel through space and time... With every exercise and every task that the "Book of Elements" presented to him, Adam's strength grew. But every day there were also moments when he realized that his abilities were still limited, because the way to Ellion was by no means without danger. Often a rider fell or a soldier fell so ill that Adam was called to help. He urgently needed to learn to weave much more magic. To heal a broken leg alone demanded so much from him that he slept through the next day before he awoke with a ravenous hunger.

After a few days they saw a city in the distance. >>There, look!<< Sven handed them a telescope. >>What you see there is Thorit, a strange city. Only crazy people live there.<< Adam suddenly had to think about his parents. I wonder what they're doing. Wonder how they were doing. But their way led past Thorit and they quickly lost sight of the city. In the night the rain began and so fire baskets were set up in the tents to keep them dry and comfortable. Adam took out his book again and joined Emiliana. Finally he had come to the page that described the Elves staff. Excited, he now took the staff in his hand and studied the engraved runes.

As instructed in the book, he woven magic around the staff and connected all the elements around it. Emiliana admired the runes, which joined together at breathtaking speed. In the middle of her tent, an image of a battlefield appeared in the smoke. Countless hordes of Shadow covered beings roared towards a herd consisting of Elves and humans. Away from it, some figures stood on a pedestal. One of them held the staff of the Elves and with united forces they directed it towards the dark army. A blue light detached itself from the staff, which spread like a net and aimed at the enemy. As soon as this light touched one of the Dangan, it was as if they were sinking into a hole in the ground. They were simply extinguished and the whole thing lasted only a few minutes. Soon the entire Dark horde was defeated.

It was quiet in the tent. Sven resolved the general rigidity by dropping his wine cup to the ground. >>That is a really very powerful weapon you carry there. I thought your sword was unique, but this staff here, it really is something else!<<

Adam tried to focus on the magic again, but the image faded. Only the staff still shines in his hand and the runes continued to connect with those on his arm. Suddenly he felt all the unbridled power of the staff, almost knocking him to the ground, almost crushing him.

Adam was no longer perceived by anyone in the tent, he was so connected to magic. He enjoyed its power. First he wanted to try changing the weather. At once the rain stopped and the stars appeared. Around the camp there was not one cloud left in the sky and it became noticeably warmer.

Emiliana scolded him >>What are you doing? Why are you wasting magic? The rain probably wouldn't have killed us.<<

Adam had used up a lot of energy, but this time he didn't feel weak or hungry. All the power did not come from him, but from the Elfin staff. In the "Book of Elements" he searched for instructions on how to store the magic in the staff. Immediately he tried to weave this magic as well and took - as described in the book - a small being to help him. The moth, which was attracted by the light of the fire, fluttered around the tent. Adam wove it under his spell and took all life energy from it. He saw a fine silver thread flowing towards the Elf's staff and disappearing with a glow inside. Although he felt sorry for the animal, the staff needed the energy.

So he had to do that with the magic he was not using. Immediately he bundled some magic and sent it into the elf's staff. The staff shone much brighter now.

They put the book away. Emiliana looked at him proudly and kissed him tenderly. This time much less weakened, he let himself sink into her arms.

Sven snored softly and right in front of him on the floor was once again a successfully emptied wine jug.

The day began with a beautiful bright morning and so everyone was in a good mood to prepare for breakfast. Only Sven still seemed to be much too tired. Emiliana thought to herself with a smile: >>How much wine might still be on the food trolleys?<< At that moment the scouts came back to the camp. One of them was seriously injured. He was quickly helped off the horse and Emiliana sent for Adam. When he saw the wound, he remembered well his own torments at the lake when they were first attacked by the Dangan. With a worried look he sat down with the soldier and while he spoke softly to him, he put his hands on the wound. The seal on his arm lit up. He could clearly feel the pain and fear that was stuck in the soldier.

A short time later, however, Adam was sitting on one of the few chairs in the camp, in front of him a large table with a map spread out on it, and the two scouts stood before him in perfect health as if nothing had ever happened. >>Report what happened. How did you get this injury?<<

The older of the two spoke softly: >>About two days from here
we rode through a small mountain ravine and saw a small fire in the distance. The one there,<< he pointed to his comrade, >>was desperate to know what the fire meant. But as we rode straight towards it, we were surrounded by the Dangan. Only with difficulty did we manage to break through their circle and escape. I suspect they were guarding a pass, because behind them I could see thousands of these beasts. If we continue in this direction, we will run straight into them.<<
Adam followed the scout's description on the map. >>It's all very well to be curious, but curiosity must not cost you your life. I am not always there to help,<< he said to the younger of the two men. >>Nevertheless, you have of course done a good job and I thank you.<<
Once again he looked at the map and now looked for a way around the Dangan. >>We want to march past their camp and overtake them, because in order to save Ellion, we have to reach the city before them! We will march by night and no longer light fires in the open sky, so that darkness hides us.<<
The other Elves hastily passed on these orders and took care of their execution.
Meanwhile Sven sat there smirking. >>Well, well, well! Now he already commands a small

master. He is doing well, the Young Sorcerer. In the end he'll be king...<< He went to pay a visit to the rest of the wine on the cart.

Early in the morning the tents were taken down and the carts loaded. Everything was in the mood for departure. With his bones still tired, Adam crept through the carts to get his horse. What would he give to finally be allowed to sleep in a real bed again or even to enjoy a hot bath.

Perhaps they would even enjoy such pleasure in Ellion?

They made headway fast. Around noon a drizzle set in, which continuously surrounded everything in a wet film. The water crept into every crack. In the distance they saw the mountains. Dark grey towered over the horizon. Ellion had to be there somewhere - and the Dangan. Adam shivered at the thought of having to face those terrible creatures again.

The path became almost impassable due to the heavy rain. Everything turned to mud and made it impossible to move forward. So they set up camp at the edge of a small forest and were relieved that the long day had come to an end.

After studying the map once more, they knew the only had one days travel left to Ellion. Kenlad pointed to a pass in the hills. It was further away than the one this road led to, but would not lead them directly into the arms of the Dangan. However, it would take them another half day longer. >>Young Sorcerer, our scout should have been back long ago.<< Adam nodded.

>>Yes, but we won't be able to wait much longer. If they are not back by daybreak, we must assume the worst and move on, because we have to get to Ellion. «

Suddenly Adam stopped, as if something had occurred to him. He gestured to Emiliana to come to him. Then he had Kenlad describe the city of Ellion and its surroundings in detail.

Only a little later he and Emiliana wove the magic together, as he had tried it before.

A new billowing hole appeared before them in the tent. Frightened, they all retreated as firestorm struck them. They saw people burning alive and heard their screams. Ellion was heavily besieged and threatened to fall if help did not come soon.

Adam closed the magic window and opened a new one. Now one could see the full extent. All the gates of the city could barely hold out and behind them there was fire everywhere. The Dangan were a huge black mass that surrounded the city.

Adam suddenly closed the window. He looked around and made a decision.

>>We are leaving, NOW! We must help the people.<< They hurriedly determined the route.

Two scouts were sent out to the right and left of the path, who were to report at regular intervals.

>>We'll camp by the pass and use the wagons to build a protective wall. Then we will attack the town from two sides. A hundred warriors head straight for it, another hundred on the flanks.<< He looked at Emiliana and Sven.

>>The three of us will attack from this hill,<< he pointed to the map, >>oversee the battle and intervene with everything we can.<<

"May the Gods be with us," sighed Sven.

Everything they didn't urgently need was left behind. Every blacksmith or servant who didn't want to fight was left behind.

Quickly they now headed for the mountains towards Ellion. On the dark horizon they could already see the glow of fire that was pouring out of the city, glowing with doom. This sight made them go even faster.

The scouts alternately reported small and large groups of Dangan guarding the road. Their plan seemed to work.

Hours later, the sky already showed the first glimmer of the morning, they reached the pass. From here, one could see the same outline of the city as before through the magic hole. The air smelled burnt. Kenlad formed the troops as instructed by Adam and let them march off. He and six other Elves knelt before the Sorcerer. "We will carry out our king's command and remain at your side." They lowered their heads.

"Stand up! We have no time for this!" Sven ran behind Emiliana and the small troop climbed one of the two hills outside the town. From here they could see the entire battlefield. They stood there as if stuck together and could not comprehend what they saw: thousands of these shadowy figures were ruthlessly pushing towards the city, destroying everything that came their way.

The first troop of Elves had already invaded the Horde and cut a swath through the ranks of the Dangan, who didn't even understand what was happening here.

Then one saw movement in the flanks and felt the unrest breaking out. The first shouts of rejoicing were heard from the city walls, and more and more tar balls and arrows were fired. The hot oil poured down on the monsters in a slow stream before they were ignited by the fire arrows. A huge wall of fire suddenly reached the sky and burned everything around it.

Adam stiffened and pressed Emiliana to himself. Before he lifted the Elf stick, he looked into her eyes and kissed her. Then he drew as much energy from the staff as he could take and directed it towards the Dangan. As they had already seen in the vision, a blue ray of light escaped from the staff, which quickly branched out and headed towards the enemy.

The air crackled. Sven watched with wide open eyes and threw the rest of the wine down his throat. Surely no human had ever seen anything like that.

As soon as the Dangan were touched by the blue light, they dissolved into nothing. Faster and faster the battlefield cleared.

Only when more than half of the Shadow Breed had been destroyed did they retreat. On the right flank a bright light suddenly flashed up and a kind of huge gate opened. The Dangan stormed towards this hole and disappeared inside.

Adam reacted quickly and sent his deadly magic towards the portal to destroy the beasts before they could disappear further inside. When the blue light reached the magic gate, the air seemed to explode. With thunderous thunder and a flash of light that for a brief moment made everything bright as day, a wave of energy struck directly in front of Adam and threw everyone far back to the ground. Even small trees flew through the air and dirt covered everything.

Then it became silent. Adam had an unbearably loud beeping in his ear and his left arm lay unnaturally twisted in front of his face. But he felt no pain. He looked for Emiliana and found only Sven. The soldier lay lifeless a few meters away from him. He had thrown himself protectively over Emiliana, who was now slowly moving and trying to free herself. Kenlad was immediately at his side. Blood ran down his face from a deep wound. Slowly his hearing was restored and only now did Adam hear that the Elf talked to him constantly. "Are you hurt? Do you need help?" The elf almost screamed now. Adam said no, let himself be helped to his feet and hurried to Emiliana who was bent over Sven worriedly. But he already opened his eyes and looked around in disbelief. "Are we dead?" he croaked and turned carefully to his side. He groped for every bone in his body. When he got up he picked up a bundle that lay beside him, took out the wine jug and took a big sip.

When they had gathered, dressed their wounds and Adam's arm straightened in a bandage, they all looked towards Ellion.

The shock wave had swept the northern city gate far into the interior of the city, causing considerable damage, but hundreds of people stood on the rubble, cheering and waving to them.

Kenlad gathered his troops. Together they set out for the city. They had arrived in time. They had made it!

The ground was soaked with dark blood and the battlefield was littered with corpses. Many brave men had died here.

From far away they realized that the soldiers started to clear the north gate and everything below it from rubble and ashes.

The high watchtower was completely tilted backwards and had buried some houses underneath.

The Elves made their way through the chaos. They were cheered and many people came and gratefully shook their hands.

In front of a very large building stood many guards, behind them King Aron. He stepped forward and greeted the rescuers of his city with a deep bow. Tears were in his eyes. You could clearly see that it was very difficult for him to find the right words.

"You are heaven-sent! You arrived just the right moment, we could not have withstood the Dangan any longer. I thank you and your soldiers for saving us. "Follow us to my castle so that our healers can see your wounds."

The part of the city through which the companions now passed was not damaged and they could easily see how rich this city was. Most of the houses were made of high quality stone and stretched over the floors and more. The streets were paved and clean. The market place of the city was gigantic. All the major streets crossed here and on every corner there were inns and shops.

A little later they arrived at the palace where they were received by a worried servant. They led Adam and all the others to a healer immediately.

Adam had not been able to heal the others, let alone himself. The struggle had strained him so much that he could hardly stand on his feet. Sunrays penetrated through the window into his room. Adam lay in a large, sumptuously decorated bed. Emiliana lay close beside him and was fast asleep.

He needed a moment. Then he suddenly remembered what had happened.

Gently he kissed his beloved on the forehead and slipped out of bed carefully and quietly so as not to wake her. After a short wash, he got dressed and set out to look for the king.

No sooner had he opened the door than the servants came running and bowed before him. "Great sorcerer, we hope you have rested well. What can we do for you?" "Take me to your king."

The footmen bowed even lower now. "Very good, sir." They led Adam down a long, high corridor. On the walls to the left and right were huge paintings of kings and warriors or even entire battlefields. Everywhere there were magnificent curtains and columns, their capitals so richly ornamented with gold that they dazzled his eyes.

In front of two big doors there were servants. They, too, bowed dutifully when they saw Adam and wordlessly opened the gate for him.

Someone announced him loudly to the king: "My king! The High Lord Sorcerer, savior of Ellion..." King Aron was a man in his forties with broad shoulders, a long beard and sad eyes, who had certainly seen many battlefields. He sat on a stately chair at a huge table, which was bent under the weight of the many dishes that were served here.

"Come, sit with me, Sorcerer. Be my guest. We have much to talk about."

King Aron beckoned him. More servants hastened to him and set a place setting and a golden goblet before him on the table. They filled the goblet with a wine that smelled deliciously of spices.

"My kingdom and I cannot thank you enough, magician. When the elf king's messenger arrived, we did not want to believe that the elves would come to our aid. We were about to abandon the city.

The door opened again. Emiliana, Sven and the Elven warriors led by Kenlad were let in and entered the hall.

Adam joyfully went to his dearest and tenderly embraced her. In astonishment he looked at Emiliana, who was wearing a dark blue dress. All around were gold lace and a wide, richly decorated belt adorned the slim waist. Adam could hardly get enough of her. "You are beautiful. You're like a princess." Embarrassed, Emiliana nudged him. He took her hand and led her to the table, and made her sit down beside him.

King Aron was still standing, now looked around and thanked everyone once again. As they ate, King Aron told them how out of the blue, out of the blue, the Dangan had suddenly appeared. Within minutes, hordes of them had appeared outside the city, as if they had grown out of the ground. By then, they were already rushing towards the city walls to destroy everything.

"Just as you intervened, these monsters took my son. All of a sudden, he just disappeared from my side, literally vanished into lust. No one could help him."

They looked at the king in dismay. Even Sven let go of his cup of wine and looked sadly at the ground in front of him while the king mourned for his son.

After the meal, everyone rode back to the north gate to survey the damage.

Countless helpers were at work here. The streets were almost completely cleared again and the gate was also recognizable as such. Only the gate house was completely destroyed and could not be saved. Some carpenters brought wood to build railings so that the city wall could be completely rebuilt.

Even women, children and wounded soldiers helped with the repairs, because the fear of the Dangan drove them all to hurry.

"We will not survive another attack. They would simply overrun us this time." King Aron remarked despondently.

Emiliana carefully tugged at Adam's jacket, pulled him aside and showed him a new page in the "Book of Elements."

Adam understood immediately. He wove his magic around the necessary elements and as if by magic, stone by stone of the city gate reassembled as if they had never been broken apart.

The workers at the gate cried out and fled in fear. King Aron looked up in amazement as the watchtower rose again and with a loud thunder came to a standing upright position where it had stood for almost a thousand years before the Dangan attack. The collapsed city wall closed again almost as quickly, and in front of it an additional rose up. Everywhere now stones and sand and water were in motion and a protective wall with a total of four city gates and gate wings of iron rose around the city.

Adam sank to the ground, completely exhausted. He knew that he had bitten off more than he could chew, but he also knew that this magic was necessary to protect the people here in Ellion.

After they had recovered from their first horror, the people could not stop thanking him. They had never seen such a miracle before.

Back in the castle he only felt the soft bed and he was already in the realm of dreams.

The next morning woke him with the smell of fried eggs and fresh bread. With an almost inhuman appetite he pounced on the food. At the table next to him Kenlad cleared his throat embarrassed so that Adam looked up at him.

"Great Sorcerer, this morning a messenger came from King Elodiron. My troops are expected back home. I, however, will remain with you with my most loyal soldiers and accompany you on your journey, if you will allow me."

Adam almost choked and finally gave Kenlad his full attention.

"But the city must be protected, Kenlad!"

"It will be, Sorverer! Your wall will do more than any Elven warrior. My king will not tolerate delay. We, too, must protect ourselves and our people from the dark forces still rampant.

Adam put his silverware aside, wiped his mouth with a cloth and stood up.

"Then we too will travel on. I gratefully accept your offer, Kenlad, and I am truly honored that you want to stay with us!"

Adam turned to Sven. "What about you, my friend? Will you join us, too?"

Sven almost dropped the wine cup from his hand. Did the Sorcerer just say "friend" to him? Hesitantly, he stood up. "Um, well, I'd have to have a word with my commander first. ...but of course I would love to go with you."

"Then it's settled," Adam cried. "I'm talking to King Aron. Will you prepare everything for your departure. We leave before noon."

In the throne room, King Aron looked with interest at the small group of people who were explaining to him verbosely what their destination was.

"I cannot stop you, that may be, but let me help you a little." He pulled out a small box of gold pieces and presented it to Adam. "Take this with you on your travels and my best horses and wagons. Take whatever staff you need. I want my best ten soldiers to go with you. And you there, soldier!" Sven winced, "Come on in!"

Hesitantly, Sven walked towards the king.

"You have shown more courage than anyone expected. You will go with him, but not as soldiers but as captains."

Sven coughed, he really hadn't expected that. His new insignia were presented to him by the King's lackeys, along with a new sword.

"I only have one last chance to thank you for saving my city. We are forever in your debt!" Sadly he added: "If you should receive any sign of life from my son on your way, I would of course be very pleased if you would report to me, for he is not only the sole heir but also my one and only.

Emiliana and Adam bowed low before the king and promised to do everything they could to find the prodigal son.

The courtyard was bustling with people, chariots were loaded and horses saddled. Sven strutted across the square in his new uniform and some of the soldiers were astonished when they saw their former comrade. They immediately saluted him. The entourage started moving and, as Adam had predicted, it was not yet noon when they left the city through the south gate.

He was determined to find the source of this dark power and end the suffering the Dangan had brought upon them once and for all.

Epilogue

First and foremost I would like to thank my family, my friends and the many helpers for the fact that this book could be published at all.
My special thanks go to the Filmclub Güstrow e. V. and the associated youth club "Alte Molkerei" as well as the "yellow fun box" youth club of the AWO Güstrow. Without you, this story would probably never have happened. Of course the spelling and grammar is horrible without proper editing, so my thanks go to Mandy Kommoß. You have done a great job. Of course, I would also like to especially emphasize the artistic achievement of Sabrina Pahlke. I thank you for the simply wonderful drawings. I would also like to thank my dear friend Maria Graumann for bringing in essential ideas and elements. My dear friend Gregor Reisch designed this wonderful cover for me. Of course I also thank you very much. Frank Waldau, many thanks also to you for the website for the book. Last but not least: Dear readers, what would this book be without you? THANK YOU!